The Aeroplane Boys Flight

by

John Luther Langworthy

The Echo Library 2007

Published by

The Echo Library

Echo Library
131 High St.
Teddington
Middlesex TW11 8HH

www.echo-library.com

Please report serious faults in the text to complaints@echo-library.com

ISBN 978-1-40681-666-2

THE AEROPLANE BOYS FLIGHT

Or A Hydroplane Roundup

CONTENTS

CHAPTER I

THE BOY FLIERS

"It was my mistake, Frank!"

"How do you make that out, Andy?"

"Simply because I was using the little patent Bird monkey-wrench last in our shop, and should have put it back in the toolbox belonging to the aeroplane. The fact that it isn't here shows that I mislaid it. Give me a bad mark, Frank."

"Well, I must say it's a queer stunt for you to forget anything, Andy Bird. But with dark coming along, and home some miles away, it's plain that we'll have to let the mending of that wing go till morning."

"But do you think, Frank, it's just safe to leave our pet hydroplane over night in this field on the Quackenboss farm?"

"Why not, Andy? Sky as clear as a bell; little or no wind promised; and then we can hire the farm hand, Felix Boggs, to keep an eye on it. Looks as easy as falling off a log."

"And all because I didn't put that little wrench where it belonged! Kick me, won't you, please, cousin; I deserve it."

"Well, I guess not. Didn't I make just as bad a break last week? I guess now, no boy's perfect. And I don't mind the walk home a bit. Fact is, it ought to do us both good, because we don't stretch our legs enough, as it is."

"You're the boss chum, Frank!"

"Then you're another. See what you get for calling me names. But when you've fastened down that plane so it can't get into trouble, if the wind should rise in the night, perhaps we'd better be hunting up this Felix Boggs, and then start for home.

"Well, I'm glad we'll get there in the night-time, Frank, even if the moon does happen to be nearly full."

"What makes you say that, Andy?"

"Because, when an aviator leaves his wounded machine in a field, and walks home, it makes him feel like a dog with his tail between his legs, sneaking along back of the fences."

Frank Bird laughed merrily at the picture drawn by his cousin and then stooping again, with a few deft turns of a heavy cord, helped Andy secure the broken plane so it would not get into trouble during the coming night.

After which the two boys headed toward the barns belonging to the farm, which just showed their tops above the adjacent rise.

While they are walking there it may be a good time for us to introduce the pair of young aviators to such readers as have not had the good fortune to meet them in previous volumes of this series of stories.

The cousins lived in the town of Bloomsbury, a thriving place situated on the southern shore of Sunrise Lake, which was a magnificent body of water, said to be nearly seventeen miles long by three wide, in places.

This lake having hilly shores that were heavily wooded in spots, and with numerous fine coves, afforded grand sport to the young people of Bloomsbury, both winter and summer.

The railroad skirted one shore and then passed through the town. Some miles off arose a lofty peak known as Old Thundertop, which had a road running part way up its side. The summit was believed to be utterly inaccessible to mortal man until one day the Bird boys managed to accomplish the wonderful feat by the aid of their aeroplane.

They had been spending all their spare time, when not in school, working upon the line that seemed to have a strange fascination for them. Frank's father was one of the best known doctors in town, a man of considerable means, and with a firm faith in his boys, so that he was easily convinced whenever Frank wished to do anything.

Andy had been living with his guardian for some time, until the return of his own father, Professor Bird, who had been lost while attempting a difficult balloon trip in Central America, and found in a most miraculous way by the two boys as told in a previous story.

Andy had inherited the passion which his father, a noted professor, had always had for navigating the air. It was a favorite expression of his "A bird by any other name would fly as high," and his cousin would retort: "A Bird takes to the air just as naturally as a duck does to water."

They had been doing some fine "stunts" during the last year or two; and it may be supposed that the people of Bloomsbury were more than a little proud of seeing the name of their town mentioned so favorably in the papers in connection with the doings of the Bird boys.

Of course, as is always the case, there was a rival in the field, who had been the cause of much trouble in the past, and still watched their work with an envious eye. This was a boy by the name of Percy Shelley Carberry, rather a bold fellow too, and as smart as they make them, only unscrupulous as to the means he employed by which to gain his ends.

Percy was the only son of a rich widow, who could never refuse him anything he demanded; and with unlimited cash at his disposal he had been able to do quite a few feats himself that might have gained him more or less fame, only that they were eclipsed by the accomplishments of Frank and Andy; and that was where the shoe pinched with Percy.

His temper was one of his weak spots, also a liking for fast life, which, of course included tippling; and the aviator who indulges to the slightest degree in strong drink is next door to a fool; for as he takes his life in his hands every time he leaves the ground, the necessity for a clear brain is apparent.

In most of his tricky work young Carberry had for a boon companion one "Sandy" Hollingshead, a sinewy chap, whose most prominent trait was his faculty for disappearing suddenly in a pinch. He was considerable of a boaster, but could always invent a most remarkable excuse for going before the storm broke. But Percy, no coward himself, knew how to make use of his sly crony;

and despite their numerous quarrels, that often ended in actual fights, the pair of precious tricksters still kept company together.

Sandy was freckled had pale eyes and very blonde hair, that gave him a queer look. Those eyes never could look any one straight in the face, but shifted uneasily; and other boys said that Sandy, the cigarette smoker, was always on the watch for a quick "getaway."

The Bird boys, of course, had many friends among the lads of Bloomsbury; but only two who were close enough to be admitted freely to the workshop on the grounds of Frank's father's place, where the young inventors worked out many of their lofty ideas.

These were Larry Geohegan, and a small runt who had been called "Elephant" by his companions in a spirit of sport, and could not shake the name. His full name was Fenimore Cooper Small, and as a rule he had always been rather timid. But Elephant was always having queer ideas in which he believed fully himself; but which were nearly always jeered at by more practical Larry.

The two Bird boys had been out on this afternoon, trying some new arrangement in connection with their hydroplane, when they met with an accident when attempting to land on the Quackenboss farm, to make some changes they saw were needed, to improve the working of the machine.

Neither of them had been even scratched, but a certain amount of damage had befallen one of the planes, which might have been remedied on the spot in time to allow them to get back home easily, only for the unfortunate fact that just when they needed a monkey wrench the worst kind, it was discovered to be missing; perhaps the only occasion when such a thing had happened with the boys.

"I just saw somebody go into the barn there," remarked Frank, as they approached the large outbuildings connected with the successful farm of Josiah Quackenboss.

"Yes, and it was the farmer himself," added Andy. "I know him pretty well; and I guess you do too, because your father brought his little boy around when everybody thought he didn't have a single chance to get well. I don't believe we'll have any trouble getting Felix Boggs to look after our machine tonight, Frank."

They quickly reached the door of the barn and could hear the steady fall of the streams of milk passing into the buckets as the farmer and his hired hand pursued the regular business of the evening.

As the two boys entered, the half grown boy started up with an exclamation of alarm, for of course both Andy and Frank looked rather queer. Each of them had on a white woolen hood that fitted close to head and shoulders, for the air in the upper currents was very cold these days, and secured to this were goggles to protect the eyes, so that they would not water and dim the vision of the aviator at just a critical instant when they needed clear sight. Then they also wore warm colored mackinaw jackets, so that altogether Felix had reason to be startled when two such "sights" suddenly entered the barn. Why, even the gentle cows showed evidence of nervousness, and came near upsetting the milk buckets.

"Hello, Mr. Quackenboss!" called out Andy, cheerfully; "we're the Bird boys, and we've dropped in on you without an invitation. The fact is, we had a little trouble with our aeroplane, and landed in your field. How much rent will you charge us, Mr. Quackenboss; to let our machine lie there over night? It needs a little fixing which we can't do until morning."

Of course Andy was joking when he said this, and the farmer knew it as well as anything. He laughed as he came around out of the stall and offered his rough hand to each of the boys.

"How are you, Andy and Frank Bird?" he said, hearty. "Say, you did give us a little start when we first saw you. D'ye know what I thought boys? Why, I was just reading in the county paper about how the bank up at Jasper was robbed by two men last week. It told how they had their faces hid back of red handkerchiefs, just like they always do out West, you know. And first thing I sighted you two, my heart nigh about jumped up in my mought, because I thought them yeggs had dropped around to see if I'd collected my monthly milk accounts in town. And about leavin' your aeroplane in my field, why, there's little that I wouldn't do for the son of the man who saved my Billie, when everybody said he'd never get well again."

"We thought you might let us show Felix here where the aeroplane lies, and that we could arrange with him to kind of keep an eye on it tonight. Of course, there isn't one chance in a thousand that anything'd happen to injure it; but then that machine represents a heap of hard work, and considerable money besides, so we don't care to take chances with it.

"Sure he can, just as well as not, eh, Felix? Suppose you go out right now, and I'll finish the milking. In the morning I want to take a look at that contraption myself. I've seen you boys sailing around more'n a little, but never got close up to examine the aeroplane. Well, I guess all the money going couldn't tempt me to go with one of you. Skip along, Felix, now."

And the farm hand, a heavy-set boy, eagerly fell in behind Frank and Andy, as, after thanking Mr. Quackenboss heartily for his kindness they passed out of the barn. Felix considered this an event in the tame routine of farm life; and would be only too glad to stay up all night, if necessary, in order to guard the precious aeroplane.

Once in the field, the boys explained to Felix what they wanted him to do, and he promised not to meddle with anything connected with the engine or the aeroplane itself.

They were passing back again toward the barns, having left their prized possession in good shape, when Andy uttered a sudden exclamation that told of both surprise and disgust.

"What's the matter now?" asked Frank, who had been talking with Felix, and was hence not so wide awake as his chum.

"Just take a look over there, and see what's stopped on the road," remarked Andy.

"Seems to be a car, and I can see two heads raised above the top rail of the fence, as if the people in it had sighted our aeroplane sprawled out there in the field, and were wondering what sort of giant insect it could be," Frank went on.

"Look closer, Frank," the other boy went on to say, while his disgust deepened; "and you'll discover that the two fellows in that car happen to be Percy Carberry and his shadow, Sandy Hollingshead. Did you ever hear of such tough luck? Of all the boys in Bloomsbury they are the last we'd want to know that we'd left our new hydroplane out, unguarded, all night, in an open field. Guess I won't go home tonight, Frank. I'd rather camp out here with Felix. You let my folks know, and turn up in the morning with a new piece for that plane. That's settled and you can't change it."

CHAPTER II

ON GUARD

"Perhaps I'd better stay with you, Andy," the other Bird boy remarked.

"No need of it," replied Andy, resolutely. "Besides, you know one of us ought to get busy in the shop, making that new piece we really need so that our job won't have to be done over again. You go, Frank. Perhaps Mr. Quackenboss would let you have a horse; or if you cared to, you give Percy a hail, and he'd take you back to town, I reckon. Goodness knows he owes you a heap, after the way you saved his life the time he was wrecked up on Old Thundertop."

What Andy referred to was a very exciting event which had occurred not so very long before, and which was fully treated in the volume preceding this.

Frank shook his head in the negative.

"I never want to ask any favor of Percy Carberry," he said, resolutely. "And if Mr. Quackenboss can't let me have a horse to ride, why, the walking is good, and I can make it in less than an hour. So don't mention that again please, Andy."

"It's too late now, anyhow," remarked the other, drily, "because there they go, spinning down the road like wildfire. Percy never does anything except in a whirl. He's as bold as they make them, and the only wonder to me is that he hasn't met with a terrible accident before now. But somehow he seems to escape, even when he smashes his flier to kindling wood. His luck beats the Dutch; he believes in it himself, you know."

"But some day it's going to fail, and then he'll never what happened to him," declared Frank. "Of all the professions in the world, that of a flying machine man is the one where a cool head and quick judgment are the things most needed. And the fellow who takes great chances, depending on his good luck, is bound to meet up with trouble. But if you are bound to stay, Andy, I'd better be off."

Upon entering the barn they found that the farmer had finished his task, and was pitching some new sweet hay to the cows.

Frank suggested hiring a horse from him, but Mr. Quackenboss scoffed at the idea.

"You're as welcome to the use of my saddle hoss as the sunlight is after a spell of rain," he said, heartily. "Here, Felix, get Bob out; and you'll find my new saddle hanging on that peg back of the harness room door. And as for Andy, who's going to stay over with us, we'll find a chair for him at the supper table, and only hope hell tell us some of the many things you two have gone through with, both around this region, and away down in South America, that time you found the lost Professor."

Inside of five minutes Frank was in the saddle, and waving his hand to his chum and cousin, of whom he was more fond than if Andy had been his own brother.

"He'd be back tonight with the part we need, and we could make home in the moonlight," said Andy, as, with the farmer he headed for the house; "only both of us have promised our folks not to travel at night-time when it can be helped. Even if the moon is bright there's always a risk about landing, because it's a tricky light at the best, and even a little mistake may wreck things. And so Frank will work in the shop tonight, and be along in the morning."

Once in the farmhouse Andy was given a chance to wash up, and then met the housewife, as well as little Billie, the small chap whose life good Doctor Bird had saved. Mrs. Quackenboss proved to be a very warm-hearted woman, and any one who answered to the name of Bird could have the very best that the place afforded. There was never a night that she did not call down the blessings of heaven upon the physician who had been instrumental in preventing her darling Billie from being taken away.

The table was fairly groaning under the weight of good things to eat, for when company comes the average farmer's wife never knows when to stop bringing out the most appetizing things to eat ever seen.

"Perhaps I'm the luckiest fellow going to be able to stay over-night with you, Mrs. Quackenboss," laughed Andy, as he sat down to the generous spread.

"Well, you know, we never like anybody to get up from our table hungry," she explained.

"The chances are that I won't be able to get up at all, for if I try to taste half I see here, I'll be foundered, as sure as anything," Andy went on to say.

The farmer was not going to allow much time to pass talking about common every-day topics. Those might do all very well when he had ordinary guests; but when fortune sent him one of the now famous Bird boys for company, he wanted to listen to some thrilling accounts of adventures that had come the way of the young and daring aviators, from the time they built their first aeroplane, after purchasing most of the parts, and found that they had an immediate rival in Percy Carberry.

Andy was willing to oblige, and kept those at the table, including the farm hand, Felix Boggs, thrilled with his stories. But the farmer could not help but notice how modest the boy was, giving most of the credit to his cousin Frank, when everybody about Bloomsbury knew that Andy deserved just as much credit, if not more, than the other Bird Boy.

After supper Andy and Felix prepared to go out to where the hydroplane lay. They meant to take blankets along, and make themselves as comfortable as possible for a night's vigil.

Andy would not have dreamed of doing this only for the fact that he knew Percy and his shadow, Sandy, were aware of the plight of the precious flier. And while Frank was inclined to partly believe that the Carberry boy might let up in his mischief-making ways for awhile at least, after all they had done for him up on Old Thundertop, Andy could not bring himself to trust the other further than he could see him. He believed that the nature of Percy was so "rotten" as he called it, that, given a chance to injure his successful rivals, he would shut his eyes to all sense of gratitude, and just lie awake nights trying to get the better of them, by fair means or foul.

Andy also knew that the other was particularly chagrined, because he did not know what manner of a new flier the Bird boys had in hand now. He had resorted to various expedients in order to find out, but all without success.

On this account, if no other, then, Andy believed that the others would be apt to come out here during the night to examine the hydroplane with the aluminum pontoons under its body for floating on the water; and perhaps to slily injure it in such a fashion that it would break down when next Frank and Andy mounted into the air.

It happened that they had alighted close to one corner of the big field, though in plain view from the pike. Andy had noted a clump of trees conveniently near, and already his mind was made up that he and Felix would camp there, to pass the night in alternately keeping watch and ward over the precious aeroplane that lay there like a wounded bird.

Felix was quivering with eagerness. This was like a picnic in the humdrum life of the farm hand. Except when the circus came to town, or there was a Harvest Home day, poor Felix knew little beyond the eternal grind of getting up before dawn, and working until long after sunset.

First of all, Andy walked around the stranded aeroplane, and took occasion to explain how it worked, using as simple language as he could find, because Felix was not at all up in professional terms, and would not have understood, had the other spoken as he might have done when talking with a fellow aviator.

Then they sought the trees, and spreading their heavy blankets so as to make as comfortable a seat as possible, started to talk in low tones.

The bright moon hung there in the sky, and it seemed as though every foot of the big meadow could be scrutinized just as well as in the daytime; but Andy knew from experience how deceptive moonlight can be, and how cautious one has to be when trying any difficult feat at such a time.

"I've heard people talk about reading by moonlight, and how they could tell a friend half a mile away," he remarked to Felix; "but let me say that it's all a humbug. There never was a brighter night than this, I reckon you'll agree with me, Felix; and yet look at that stump not a stone's throw away; you couldn't say now whether it was a cow lying down, a horse, a rock, or a stump, which last I take the thing to be. Am I right about that."

"Why, sure's I live, that ere is a fact, Andy," replied the other; "but I never'd a thought it. Moonlight fools a feller the worst kind. I throwed a stone at a whippoor-will as was perched on the roof a-keepin' us all awake nights, and would yuh believe me, she went right through the winder of the attic, kersmash. Never was more surprised in my life. And you don't ketch me heavin' stones by moonlight agin."

From one subject they drifted to another. Andy even told more or less about how Percy Carberry had hated and envied them in the past, and how often he had tried to do them a serious injury.

"Frank seems to think he will give up that mean sort of play, because we really saved his life that time we had our race to the rock on the summit of Old Thundertop, and his aeroplane was smashed there; so one of us had to carry Percy and Sandy home, bruised as they were. But I don't, because I know it'd take more than that to change the spots of a fellow of his kind. And chances are, Felix, we'll find those two boys sneaking up here before the middle of the night."

"Wish't they would," chuckled the farm hand. "You're ready to give 'em a warm time of it, I guess, Andy. Be as good as any old circus to me, just to see how they jump when you open up. Let 'em come, says I. The sooner the better, too."

Long they lay there, and talked in low tones. Felix wanted to make the best of this glorious chance. A new world seemed to open up to the farm hand, as he heard of the wonderful things the Bird boys had seen, and taken part in. Perhaps ambition was beginning to awaken in the boy's soul, and he might not after this be so satisfied to plod along in the same old rut every day of the year. Perhaps the seed thus sown might take root, and bring him either great good or harm, as the tide of fortune chose.

"We heard as how a feller was up there to watch you boys fly not a great while ago, Andy," he went on to say; "an' he was so took by the way you managed things that he wanted to get you to go in with a big concern run by a boss airman; but you just up and told him you couldn't do that same. Was that so?"

"Why, yes, you must mean Mr. Marsh," returned the other, modestly. "I believe he did read some account of us that got into the papers, and was sent up here to look us up. He was kind enough to compliment Frank on the way he made that corkscrew climb; and also on his volplane drop; said we had both of them down pretty fine; and he did hint at our having a chance to go in with his company; but of course we couldn't think of that. We're too young to dream of being professional fliers yet; and besides, we've got to go to school again pretty soon. So we turned the offer down. But Mr. Marsh was mighty kind, and we liked him a heap."

"Heard how he was watching you fly, when that little chap belonging to Cragan, the fisherman, got overboard, out in the lake; and this same gent, he saw Frank dive right off his aeroplane like a bullfrog, and save little Tommy. That jest took him by storm, he told Mr. Quackenboss, and he meant to get you boys for his company if money could do it, but it all ended in smoke, didn't it."

It was almost half past nine before Andy decided that the time had come for them to shut up shop, and do no more talking.

"I'm going to take the first watch myself, Felix, and I promise to wake you up when I get to gaping, whether it's midnight or two in the morning," he said, as he settled himself more comfortably on his blanket, and pulled it up over his shoulders, because the night air was already quite chilly, and would undoubtedly be much more so ere long.

"But chances air, Andy, they're a-goin' to come inside an hour or so; and you must promise to give me a kick, if so be I'm sleepin', then. You will, won't you?"

"Sure," replied the Bird boy. "After you being so kind as to keep me company, I'd never think of making a move, and you asleep. So just settle down, and don't get excited if you feel me pushing my toe into your ribs later on."

Felix was tired from his day's work. He had probably been constantly busy since four the morning before. It was therefore a fight between weary muscles and brain, and the desire to stay awake, in order to see all that went on.

This lasted for perhaps ten minutes.

Then Andy knew that Nature had won out, for he could catch the regular breathing of the stout farmhand, and from this judged that Felix must be sound asleep.

From where Andy sat he had a fine view of the field on all sides of the broken hydroplane, and especially in that quarter toward the fence, beyond which the road leading to Bloomsbury lay.

He kept up a constant watch, never relaxing his vigilance for a single second, for Andy knew that while one might be on guard for fifty-nine minutes, if he relaxed just for a breath, that was almost sure to be the time when something would happen. How often he had proved that when fishing, and taking his eye from his float just to glance up at some passing bird, when down it would bob, and he had missed a chance to hook a finny prize.

The time passed on.

Three separate times did Andy look at his little dollar nickel watch, and in the bright moonlight he could see that it was now after eleven. He was beginning to believe that if there was anything doing that night, it must come about very soon, when he thought he heard a sound down the road that made him think a car that had been coming along had stopped short.

Thrilled with the expectation that a change was about to occur, he sat up a little more eagerly, and continued to scan the line of fence, as well as the field lying between the road and the helpless hydroplane.

CHAPTER III

NOT CAUGHT NAPPING

Five, ten minutes passed.

Andy was beginning to fear that after all he had been mistaken, and that it had been some other sound he had heard when he thought a car had stopped down the road toward Bloomsbury.

Then all at once he detected a movement over at the fence, and the figure of a man or boy was seen to quickly clamber over, dropping in the field. Even as he looked a second followed suit, then a third and even a fourth.

"Whew! what's all this mean?" Andy whispered to himself, as he took notice of the fact that there was quite a procession of fellows changing base from the road to the field: "Percy and Sandy thought they might need help in their little game of smashing our machine, or carrying it off somewhere, so as to give us a bad scare; and I reckon they've picked up a couple more of the same kind as themselves. Well we ought to be able to take care of four just as easy as two 5 and the howl will be all the louder, I guess."

He moved over a little, and with the toe of his shoe nudged Felix under the ribs.

"Quit shovin' there!" muttered the farm hand, possibly thinking he was in bed with some other boy.

Luckily the night breeze was making the windmill turn, not very far away; and as it needed oiling, there was a constant succession of squeaks and groans; so that the chances of Felix being heard when he spoke in this way were very small. Andy would not take any further risk but creeping over shook the boy roughly.

"Wake up, Felix; they're coming across the pasture!" he whispered in his ear.

That was quite enough for Felix. He seemed to grasp the situation at once, and only muttering the one significant word, "Gosh!" he immediately sat up.

Andy, moving as little as possible, pointed to where moving figures could just be detected advancing in a bent-over attitude.

"How many?" whispered the farm hand.

"I counted four," replied the other.

"Whee! bully for that!" chuckled Felix, no doubt tickled because the promised circus would be a double-ring affair, instead of the ordinary kind, and therefore quite up to date.

Both of them lay there watching intently.

They could see how the intruders were crawling along, anxious apparently only to avoid being seen from the direction of the farmhouse, the roof of which showed dimly in the moonlight over on the other side of the little ridge.

As the creepers drew closer, the watchers saw that they had adopted the method spoken of by the farmer in connection with the bank thieves, keeping their identity secret—they all seemed to have handkerchiefs tied across their faces, and kept their hats pulled well down, so that they could easily have passed close to an acquaintance without much risk of discovery.

Of course Andy could tell that they were boys, and not men; and it was an easy task for him to guess who two of the party at least must be.

The preparations he and Felix had made were about as simple as anything could be. The farm hand possessed an old musket that had been used in the Civil war, and which, muzzleloader that it was, had probably brought down many a plump rabbit when held in the hands of the owner, as well as black ducks in the marshes along the shore of Lake Sunrise.

Besides this, the farmer had loaned Andy his double-barrel Marlin shotgun, an old model when compared with the up-to-date hammerless and the repeaters, but no doubt a good, serviceable weapon.

Of course they had no idea of trying to pepper the marauders, though it would seem as though they richly deserved to be punctured with a few small bird shot, because of the meanness of their contemplated action.

To give them a good fright would satisfy Andy, and he had made the eager farm hand promise to fire up in the air also because he was afraid lest Felix allow his indignation to have full swing, when he saw what the four boys meant to do.

They were skulking very close to where the aeroplane lay now, and the critical moment had undoubtedly arrived when the surprise must be launched.

"Ready, Felix!" he whispered, in the softest of tones.

"Yep!" grunted the farm hand, at his elbow.

"One, two, three! Blaze away!"

With the last word Felix let go with his old musket, into which he must have rammed a tremendous charge, for it made a report like unto the crash of thunder, and came very near sending the owner flat on his back.

Immediately on the heels of this boom Andy pulled one of the triggers of his double-barrel, so that the report seemed almost merged in with that of the other weapon.

The four boys had jumped to their feet at the flash and report which startled them when Felix fired. And as they turned to dash wildly away and that second shot came, they became madly excited, evidently under the full belief that they were being made targets for a whole battalion of sharpshooters.

Two of them collided, and rolled over on the grass, kicking wildly and scrambling to their feet again, to resume their flight toward the fence, which doubtless seemed three times as distant as when they were creeping toward the stranded aeroplane.

The whole thing was so ridiculous that Andy burst out laughing, and could hardly hold his gun; seeing which the farm hand made bold to snatch it out of his hands, and aiming directly at the place where the fugitives were just then in the act of mounting the fence in their panicky flight, he pulled the trigger.

There was a series of loud yells, which would seem to indicate that a few of the small shot contained in the shells with which the Marlin had been loaded must have reached their mark, and pricked the boys like so many needles would have done.

That was the last seen of them, though for a short time they could be heard running along the hard road, and exchanging excited comments, possibly comparing their injuries.

Then a car was heard to start off with a great deal of bluster, and came dashing along past the farmhouse, though those in it bent low enough to keep any one from discovering who they might be.

Andy did not know whether to be a little angry or not because of what the impetuous Felix had done, but apparently nobody had been seriously hurt; and on the whole, the four "sneaks," as Felix called them, deserved some punishment; so he let it go at that.

There was no further alarm that night. Neither of the guardians of the hydroplane expected any, after the prompt measures that had been taken to inform meddlers of the warm reception they might expect.

All the same, Andy kept up his vigil until sleep almost overpowered him, when he aroused Felix to finish out the night.

With the coming of early dawn he knew that the safety of the imperiled aeroplane was assured, and that when the horn blew, he and Felix could both go in to breakfast. Indeed, he released the farm hand long before that time, so that he might go about his usual early morning chores; and Andy himself found plenty to do around the machine until summoned to the morning meal.

The farmer was a hard sleeper, and had not heard a single thing that had taken place; so that he was surprised when told how the enemy had come after all, and what measures the boys had taken in order to frighten them away.

He even told Felix he could have a day off as soon as the last load of hay was in the barn, just to show how he appreciated the bold way in which his hired help had tickled the rascals when they were getting over the fence. Indeed, the farmer said Andy had been too lenient, and that if it had been his aeroplane that was threatened in that mean way, he would have felt wholly justified in emptying both barrels of the gun after the marauders, first giving them time to get a certain distance off, so that no serious results might follow the discharge.

But Andy was never a vindictive lad, and he believed the fellows had received sufficient punishment, especially as no one knew exactly what they had meant to do in connection with the new hydroplane. Possibly Percy only wanted to look it over at close quarters, and knowing he would not be allowed to do so if he asked permission outright, sought to take this opportunity. But from the way in which they had rigged themselves out, so as to avoid being recognized, if seen, it looked as though the four boys had something more than that in view.

However, all's well that ends well, and Andy was quite satisfied with the way things had turned out.

"Here's hopin' a few of 'em may be limpin' 'round this same mornin', and feelin' rayther stiff in the legs," Felix took occasion to remark, as they sat at table, and Andy was again in danger of being foundered by the multitude of good things which the farmer's wife spread thereon, bacon and eggs, fried potatoes, scrapple, puffy biscuits, apple sauce, doughnuts, cold pie, jelly, and finally heaping dishes of light pancakes, which were to be smothered in butter and real maple syrup made on the farm each early spring when the sap was running.

"I expect Frank will be along any minute now," Andy remarked, about the time he had to firmly refuse a fourth helping of cakes, because he could hardly breathe comfortably. "It wouldn't take him long to do what little work was necessary, in our shop, which you know my old guardian, Colonel Whympers, built for us before we found my father, when he was marooned in that valley in South America, a prisoner for many months, because the cliffs around prevented him from escaping. And of course he'll gallop out here on your saddle horse, Mr. Quackenboss."

"Well, work ain't got any call on either Felix or me until we see all that goes on, that's flat," remarked the farmer, with a smile, "and it's lucky he done the milkin' already, or else the cows'd have to wait long after their usual hour, which is a bad way to treat 'em, you know."

They all went out to the field, even the housewife and little Billie wanting to see what a real aeroplane looked like at close quarters. Many times had all of them seen the Bird boys, and perhaps Percy Carberry as well, soaring aloft as if the upper air currents might be their natural heritage; but up to now they had never had the chance to examine one of the wonderful machines, and touch the various parts gingerly as though afraid of injuring them.

"Beats all what people are a-doing nowadays," ventured the farmer, shaking his head with astonishment, almost awe, as he looked the thing over. "They ain't even contented to just fly like a red-tailed hawk, or an eagle that kin look the sun direct in the eye; but now they got to have a contraption that's at home in the air or on the water; a hydroplane you called, it didn't you, Andy? And them ere twin pontoons underneath, that look kinder like gondolas, as you say, are made of aluminum, and kin hold up the whole affair when you light on water. But tell me, how in all creation kin you ever mount up agin, once you settle there?"

"Why that's the easiest thing of all," replied the young aviator; "you've watched a wild duck get up many a time, haven't you, Mr. Quackenboss; well, we do just the same, only instead of flapping our wings, we start the engine, and skim along the surface for a little distance, then elevate the planes, and immediately begin to soar upward. And it does the stunt as gracefully as anything you ever saw. Some time I hope to give you a chance to see how it works. When we leave here, of course we'll use the bicycle wheels you see underneath, and run along the ground until going fast enough to soar. But I think I see Frank coming, away down the road there."

"That's right," declared the farmer; "I know my Bob as far as I can see him, and his gallop in the bargain."

Frank was evidently coming at full speed, and Andy presently got the idea in his head that his cousin seemed to be strangely in a hurry for him. He wondered whether anything could have happened at home, and if Frank would prove to be the bearer of bad news.

The other dashed into the narrow road leading from the pike to the barns of the Quackenboss farm. Hitching the horse to a post, he started toward the spot in the big field where the two boys and the farmer awaited his coming, close beside the stranded aeroplane.

Frank was carrying the little part he had expected to knock together at the workshop; but as he drew nearer, his chum could readily see that he was considerably excited.

"Is everything all right here, Andy?" he called out, even before reaching them.

"Yes," replied the other Bird boy, promptly, "though we did have a call from four fellows who had their faces hidden behind handkerchiefs, but we fired our guns in the air and nearly frightened them to death. Felix grabbed the double-barrel I had, and gave them a last shot when they were climbing the fence over there; and we heard some howls too, so I guess a few of the Number Eight shot pinked them. But what makes you look so bothered, Frank? Has anything happened at home?"

"There sure has," came from Frank, as he joined them, and cast a pleased glance over the flying machine that lay upon the grass like a huge bat, with wings extended.

"Tell me what it was?" demanded Andy, breathlessly.

"Somebody broke into our hangar and workshop, and knocked things around at a great rate," Frank went on to say. "Acted like they might be just mad because they didn't find our new machine there, and wanted to show their spite. And nobody in your house knew a thing about it till I came along, after an early breakfast, meaning to get the piece I'd been working on up to eleven last night, when I went home to sleep, and locked up the place as usual."

"That's a queer piece of news you're telling me, Frank," said the other, looking puzzled, as well he might.

CHAPTER IV

THE STARTLING NEWS

"Well," said Frank, with a frown on his face. "It's puzzled me a whole lot, let me tell you, Andy. Because, of course, my first thought was that it must have been Percy Carberry's work; but now that you tell me he was here, and knew we hadn't fetched our hydroplane home, I hardly know what to think."

"Did you say you worked till about eleven at the shop?" asked Andy, quickly.

"Three minutes after when I quit, locked up, and went home," Frank replied.

"That was just about the time they showed up here," the other went on to say. "Unless one of us is wrong about the time, they couldn't well be in two places at the same minute, now, could they? Seems like it might have been some other crowd that broke into our hangar, Frank!"

"But why? Did they want to play fast and loose with our machine, and force an entrance just for that purpose? Listen to something I'm going to tell you, Andy. I found several things on our work bench where somebody had left them, without meaning to do it, I guess. Here's one."

Frank while saying this held something up which he had taken from the package he carried under his arm.

"Why, that's a splendid electric torch, looks like to me?" exclaimed Andy.

"Just what it is, now," the other agreed.

"And it was forgotten in our shop, was it?" demanded Andy.

"I made out that whoever entered used this first, and then lighted our lamp to look around with, putting out the torch, and laying it down. When they skipped out, why, they just forgot all about it, also these."

Again did Frank make a dive into his pocket, and dangled something before the astonished eyes of his cousin.

"Great Caesar! what d'ye call those things?" gasped Andy, staring as though hardly able to believe his eyes.

"Well, as near as I can make out, they're a couple of half masks made out of black muslin, and just like a domino worn at a masquerade ball." Frank remarked, with positive conviction in his voice and manner.

"Masks?" echoed the other; "and the fellows who broke open our shop wore them, did they? Well, the crowd that came out here seemed to be satisfied to tie handkerchiefs across their faces, and pull their hats down."

"I don't know that they wore them," Frank went on, "but they had the things along and laid them down with the lantern, forgetting the whole lot when they cleared out. Perhaps your dog got to barking and frightened them off before they found a chance to do much damage."

"A regular bullseye electric torch, and black masks like cracksmen use—say, tell me, Frank, what's coming over our quiet country up here lately? There was the affair over in a neighboring town, when yeggmen broke into the bank, and robbed it; and now here you tell me we've had a little smash-up on our own account, with the burglars leaving cards behind them. But what d'ye think now anybody would want to go poking around in our shop for, Frank?"

His cousin was looking very grave.

"Well, you forget that we've been working overtime this winter on several little inventions that, if we ever complete them, will make a stir in the world of aviation."

"Jupiter, I had let that slip away from me, for a fact, Frank!" exclaimed the other, looking rather startled.

"Of course, it sounds pretty big for us to even imagine that any party could take enough interest in what the Bird boys are doing to come up here, intending to break into the shop, and learn our secrets; but what else can we think, tell me that, Andy?"

"But they wouldn't find out much, even if they had six hours to poke around our shop in, would they, Frank?"

"I guess you're right, because we've made it a rule to be cautious enough to hide our work and cover our tracks as we go along. But let's get busy now, and put the plane into shape, so we can slip along home. And as we work we can keep on talking as much as we want to," Frank went on to say.

The farmer and Felix still loitered around, determined to see the wonderful contrivance make a start, and expecting the greatest treat of their lives, when that event occurred.

Such experienced workers as the two Bird boys had now become would find little or no trouble about carrying out the work they had on hand. Every steel wire guy was kept as taut as a fiddle string; and by the time they were done handling the aeroplane it would be in apple-pie shape for work.

"Did they smash much in the shop, Frank?" Andy asked after they had been working some little time, and making fair progress.

"Why, no, it didn't seem to me that they took the time to do great damage; and that's why I fancy they were scared off, somehow or other. They went in a hurry, or else they would never have forgotten those things. And when I looked around I made up my mind that they were just mad because they didn't find our machine at home, and so tried to let us know that fact."

"Perhaps it was a second detachment of the same crowd that came out here?" suggested Andy, speculatively.

"Tell me, what would they be doing with electric torches, and black masks? Now, you can see that these have been pretty well used; they're not new ones just cut out by pattern at home with mother's scissors. These have been made by an experienced operator, and were bought either for a mask ball or some other purpose."

"Well, perhaps we'll never know the truth about it," grumbled Andy, who never liked anything to puzzle him and would lie awake half the night trying to find the answer to a conundrum that had been offered to him by a boy friend.

"Oh! yes, I've got a hunch that we will," chirped his cousin, with a sublime confidence that quite won Andy's heart; if he could not see any good reason for hope himself, the fact that his chum pinned his faith on it was enough to bolster up his own courage.

Meanwhile they were both as busy as bees, and the work was approaching completion.

"What are you looking up every little while that way for?" Frank asked, after noticing that Andy cocked his eye upward several times, and appeared to be scanning the heavens in an expectant manner; "the day is all right, so far as wind goes, and we ought to get along home without a bit of trouble."

"Oh! I wasn't bothering my head about that part of it," the other replied, with a scornful smile. "We've been out in all sorts of weather; and now that we have a chance to try this new invention of the Wrights', that makes it next to impossible to tilt an aeroplane over no matter how you move around when up in the air, we can feel safer than ever. Even a fool would be kept from meeting with an accident when protected by that wonderful balancing bar that responds to the slightest movement of the human body."

"Then it was something else you had on your mind, was it, Andy?"

"Well, I was wondering just what took Percy and Sandy out at daybreak this morning, that's all," replied the other.

"What's that? Did you see them pass over in their biplane this morning?" demanded the other.

"Felix woke me up at dawn to tell me there was a queer chugging overhead, that sort of scared him. I jumped up, because of course I knew what that must mean. And sure enough I was just in time to see a biplane pass over at a good height, and head up the lake. I lost it back of the barn, because a flock of crows came flying along, stretching out for a mile or two; and among the lot I couldn't make out just what was biplane and which was crow. It was pretty high up, too, I thought."

"But you made sure it was Percy's biplane?" asked Frank, interested somewhat, for somehow the other rival flier was always doing such bold stunts that he could not help feeling as though it might pay to keep track of what he was doing, lest their interests clash unexpectedly, in midair perhaps.

"I ought to know the way it glides, and the whole general look; and I'd be willing to take my affidavy that was the Canvas-back, as he calls his biplane."

"And he was in it, of course, with Sandy too?" Frank went on.

"I could just make out that there were two aboard," said Andy, "but somehow it seemed to me that Percy had altered his whole way of piloting his airship, or else he was drunk, and hardly knew what he was doing."

Frank whistled to indicate his surprise and consternation:

"When it gets as rough as that you can take it from me that Percy's mother will hear something simply awful about him before long. He's bound to go from bad to worse; and everybody knows what the end of such an aviator is going to be."

"But what under the sun could he be off at daylight this morning for?" Andy went on to remark, as though that thing had been bothering him ever since the moment he lost track of the biplane among the teetering, cawing crows.

Frank shrugged his shoulders as he replied:

"Did you ever know any reason for half the things Percy does? He just acts from a sudden impulse. Remember all that happened when he followed us down there to Columbia in South America, and tried to give us all the trouble he could make up. And there have been lots of other times too, we can look back at, all of which prove what I am saying that he is often like a ship without a rudder. Now, perhaps, he's got the crazy notion in his head that we might prosecute him either for what he tried to do up here to our hydroplane, or on account of breaking into our hangar, and doing a certain amount of damage, if the vandal was Percy Carberry."

"That sounds a little reasonable, anyhow, Frank. Queer that I never seem to get hold of these things, and they just float along as easy as anything to you. But it looks as if we had her all primed up now as steady as a church. How about it, Frank?"

For answer the other touched several taut wire guys with a peculiar little movement of finger and thumb, and each one responded with a musical note that was the sweetest possible sound in the responsive ear of the young aviators.

"All done, and let's be off," he said, presently, after the last test had been applied.

Accordingly they shook hands with Farmer Quackenboss, his good wife, and Felix, in the palm of which latter Andy made sure to leave a greenback that made the boy grin broadly.

Three minutes later Frank sang out the word, and both the farmer and Felix ran along with the machine for a dozen paces or so, when it left them behind, taking on speed, and finally rushing over the ground at a tremendous pace.

Uptilting the planes caused it to leave the ground and start to curve gracefully upward, as the whizzing propeller did its noisy duty.

They could hear the farmer and his hired hand shouting themselves hoarse with delight at having actually witnessed the start of a modern aeroplane; but naturally the sound grew fainter and fainter in their ears as they left the field and the squatty farmhouse far behind.

Having arisen to the height of several hundred feet, Frank headed toward Bloomsbury. Like a true and alert pilot he was watching and listening to ascertain how their recent work held; and presently a satisfied expression crossing his face announced that he found his faith well justified.

They had skimmed along for perhaps a mile or more when Andy made a certain discovery that caused him to call out.

"Look along the road below and ahead, Frank," he said, "and you'll see something that makes you think of old times, when we hunted, in company with Chief Waller, for those men who looted Leffingwell's jewelry establishment."

"Why, as sure as you're born, Andy, it does look like the Chief; and he's sitting in a vehicle, waving his hat. He seems to be looking up at us, and now that I've turned off the motor to glide a little I can hear him shouting."

"Frank, do you think he's just saluting us, or does he want us to come down?" demanded Andy, in some apprehension.

"Now he's making all sorts of gestures, and honestly I think he means that he wants to see us. Had we better drop in that open field just alongside the road? Looks good to me for a rise when we want to start again."

"Whatever you think best, Frank; I'm always willing to be guided by you. Mighty seldom you make a bad mess of it, while I often do. Yes, let's drop down, and if the field turns out to be pretty smooth, we'll land."

Accordingly, the hydroplane which was of course now in a condition for making a landing with the wheels below the aluminum pontoons, circled around, dropping lower and lower, until presently it came to a stop in the field close to the fence.

When it landed it was done so beautifully that, as Andy enthusiastically said, an egg would hardly have broken had it come between. And there, not more than twenty feet away, the man, dressed in a blue uniform and wearing a silver shield with the words "Chief of Police" engraved upon it, was soothing his horse, which had apparently been badly frightened by the swooping down of what seemed to be a great roc, or some other species of now extinct gigantic kings of the air.

"What's up, Chief?" asked Frank, as soon as they had reached the road together.

"Then you haven't heard the terrible news; they told me you left home to come up here about daybreak; and we didn't find it out until an hour ago. The bank in Bloomsbury was broken open last night, the safe rifled, and the thieves have disappeared in the queerest way ever heard of, for they left no trace behind. And when I saw you boys aloft, I was in hopes you might have seen something of the bank looters."

CHAPTER V

THE EXCITEMENT GROWS

"Well, what d'ye think of that for news, eh, Frank?" burst out Andy, in his usual impetuous way, after the Bloomsbury Chief of Police had made this startling announcement.

Frank was as a rule much cooler than his cousin. He had undoubtedly been equally astounded to hear of the terrible calamity that had befallen the banking institution, in which most of the leading citizens of the town were financially interested; but he certainly did not show it the same way.

His eyebrows went up to indicate astonishment; and a slight frown settled on his grave face, as he replied to Andy's question.

"It's a stunner, just as you say, Andy; but I wish the Chief would tell us a few more details. I think it's a little queer nobody seemed to have any suspicion of this awful business at the time I left home on horseback, to ride up to the Quackenboss farm, where you had been watching our injured aeroplane all night."

"Well," continued the head of the Bloomsbury police force; "that's because the yeggs worked so neatly they never left a bit of mess around to arouse suspicion; and the first thing that was known of the looting of the bank was when Seth Jarvie, the day watchman, went into the place at seven this morning to relieve Cadger, the night man, and found him lying there, tied up like a bundle of goods, and nearly dead with fright and humiliation."

"Whew!" was the way Andy relieved his pent-up feelings at this point; while his cousin went on asking questions.

"Then Cadger must have seen the robbers, if they captured him; how about that, Chief?" he demanded, eagerly; for the excitement was beginning to take hold of him.

"That's right, he did, and was able to give us more or less information," the police officer continued. "Of course as soon as Jarvie saw what had happened he knew it was a case for me to handle, and so he ran across to Headquarters; and in a jiffy we had thrown a cordon of police around the building to keep out the curious citizens who would have no business inside, and spoil any trace of the rascals."

"And would you mind telling us what Cadger had to tell, Chief?" asked Frank.

"Not at all, because I'm depending on you boys to help run the thieves down, if you feel like giving the authorities any assistance," the other replied, craftily.

Frank's answer was immediate and to the point.

"Of course we'll do anything that's in our power, Chief. Both our fathers are interested in that bank; and besides, the good name of the town must suffer if it is wrecked by a wandering band of yeggmen. And we can understand why you should want to capture the thieves, Chief; because that's a part of your business. Please tell us what the bank watchman had to say."

"Then I will, and without any frills, if I can make it that way," returned the other earnestly. "Cadger says he was caught napping, not that he was asleep; but never dreaming of any danger, he stepped over to the door when he heard a knock and a voice said: 'It's me, Cadger, Mr. Hedden, the cashier; I forgot some important papers, and have gotten out of bed to come back for them. Let me in without attracting any attention, if you can.'"

"What do you think of the smartness of that?" exclaimed Andy. "And so of course poor old Cadger, who is as honest as the day is long, never suspected any trick, but went and opened the door a crack?"

"Just what he did," returned the Chief, "and as that side of the bank was in the shadow he could only see the figure of a man, who slipped in alongside him. Before he knew what was happening he was being chocked by a pair of strong hands. Cadger started to struggle but another man must have joined the first, for he was knocked unconscious by a cruel blow, that's left his face all bloody and after that he didn't know a thing for an hour or two."

"Whee! you've got me all worked up with your story, Chief," said Andy again. "I can just seem to see the whole thing happening. And chances are, that when Cadger did come to, he found himself tied up, and unable to even whisper?"

"He had hard work to get enough breath, they had fastened the bandage across his mouth so tight; but he could see out of one eye. And lying there, Cadger watched the two yeggs go through the whole operation of getting nitroglycerine planted, and using all sorts of clothes and even the rugs off the floor of the president's room to deaden the sound of the explosion."

"They were old hands at the business, that's sure," remarked Frank, when the officer paused to catch his breath; for he was talking unusually fast in his desire to give them all the particulars in as brief a space of time as possible.

"Yes, there can be no doubt of that," the Chief went on to say, wagging his head wisely; "and they had been able in some way to get on to a lot of things that make us wonder like the name of the cashier and the night-watchman. Looks mighty much like they must have had a friend around Bloomsbury, who put them wise to those facts. Then they seemed to have the running of the trains down pat also; for long after they had their arrangements made they just sat down and waited until the freight going north and passing Bloomsbury at two-eighteen was pounding up-grade from Deering's Crossing, and making all manner of noise."

"Oh! to think of the smartness of that, would you?" burst out Andy. "I was wondering how they could blow open the safe, and the sound of the explosion never even be heard over at Headquarters, only half a block away; but now I see how it could be done. Just like a fellow says he can pull a hair out of your head, and you not feel it; and he makes out to give you a thump on the head with his other hand at the same time, so of course you never notice him pulling the hair."

"Just about on the same principle," said the officer, nodding; "for when that heavy freight goes pounding past the station, it makes enough noise to drown almost any sort of sound. The windows rattle, and we always have to stop talking until the caboose gets past. And that was the time they chose to explode their juice, with an absolute certainty that no policeman's ear would hear a single thing."

"And Cadger saw it all, did he?" asked practical Frank.

"A good lot of it, by twisting his head from time to time," replied Chief Waller. "And after the thing had been successfully done, he could watch the two thieves gathering the swag together, and putting it in a satchel they found in the cashier's room. Then, just at a quarter to three they doused the glim, which was only an electric torch one of them carried, and skipped out, locking the door on poor Cadger. It was hours afterwards when the day watchman came on duty and the discovery followed."

Frank and Andy had somehow turned, and exchanged a significant look about this time; and the expression of astonishment on the face of the latter deepened.

"Did you say an electric torch, Chief?" demanded Frank, immediately.

"Yes, one of the handy kind that are used so commonly now," the other replied.

"Tell us, did Cadger say anything about the thieves wearing masks over their faces; or did they use handkerchiefs to hide them from him?"

"I didn't mention that matter, but it was just as you say, Frank; both men had on masks all the time," answered the police officer.

"Black ones too, I expect?" ventured Andy.

"That's what they were; but see here, are you two just guessing this, or do you happen to know something about those men?" asked the other, quickly; for he could not help seeing from the manner of the Bird boys that they were on some sort of a scent; and he knew from past experiences that their sagacity could always be trusted to do the right thing.

"Well," Frank went on to say, drily, "while Andy was watching our new hydroplane out in the Quackenboss pasture, I worked until eleven o'clock in our shop, and then went home. This morning, early, after a bite to eat, I hurried over there to do some finishing touches and carry the thing out to apply to our broken plane, when to my astonishment I found that the shop had been broken into later in the night, as well as our hangar, where the aeroplane is usually kept. And here's what I discovered lying on the work-bench, where the men had forgotten them."

With these words he held up the flashlight torch, and the twin black masks; and they produced an immediate shock upon the Chief of Police.

"And you found those things in your workshop this morning, you say?" he cried, reaching out to take hold of the torch, and the bits of black muslin.

"Yes, and whoever was there, they must have been mad because they didn't find the aeroplane, for they smashed a few things, just for spite, it looked like," was what Frank added.

"Then, if it was the same men who robbed the bank they must have known about you boys having a brand new machine. And say, that must mean one of the robbers was something of a birdman himself; because no greenhorn would ever think of making his getaway in an aeroplane. Don't you see that's a pretty good clue, Frank? I'll remember that when I'm getting in touch with other points, and find out if there's any aviator who's gone crooked of late. Yes, that's worth knowing, now; and I'm glad you mentioned it to me."

"What description did Cadger give of the men, Chief?" queried Frank.

"Oh! he said one was tall and thin; and the other short and wiry like, pretty much like a cat. I rather reckon he'd be the fellow who's been in the flying business. Seemed to have a stiff left arm too, like he'd met up with some sort of an accident. That might turn out to be a pointer; I'll just remember it. It surely was a lucky thing for me I saw you boys come sailing along and managed to attract your attention. I begin to feel better already. You gave me so much help on that other occasion, it just seems as if I had to fall back on you again."

"Better move your horse out of the way, Chief, because there comes a car at a licketty-split racing speed. Wonder what the fellows in it are thinking about, to take such chances. Why, hello! look there, Frank, perhaps you know the one who's at the wheel? Seems to me I've seen him before, and that his name is Percy Carberry."

"It is Percy," said Frank, "and alongside him who'd you expect to see but his shadow, Sandy Hollingshead? And they look some excited too, as though they'd heard about the robbery, and the Carberry family was threatened with bankruptcy if the missing funds were not recovered right away. There, he sees us, and is pulling up. I reckon he's looking for you, Chief."

The car that had been tearing along the pike came to a stop close to where the head of the Bloomsbury police force sat in his buggy.

Percy Carberry got out, and Andy could not but notice that he was not displaying his accustomed agility on this fine morning; indeed, he made a face as though it gave him a stab of pain every time he took a step.

"Hello! Chief Waller!" remarked Percy in his customary patronizing way, ignoring the presence of the Bird boys completely and purposely, of course; "I've come out after you, to get your assistance in trying to find the rascals who broke into my hangar some time last night, and ran away with my biplane!"

Upon hearing these astonishing words it was little wonder that Andy and Frank once more looked at each other, with the light of understanding dawning on their faces.

CHAPTER VI

FIGURING IT ALL OUT

"That's a strange story you're telling us, Percy," said the Head of the local police force, at which the boy bridled up immediately.

"I don't see what there is so funny about it, Chief!" he exclaimed, frowning. "I tell you my hangar was broken open last night, and I'm out a biplane that cost me a good round sum. It's up to you to get on the track of the same, and recover it. I hereby offer a reward of three hundred dollars for the recovery of my machine uninjured, and make it five hundred if the thief is captured in the bargain."

When he said this Percy assumed all the airs of a millionaire; but then it was well known about Bloomsbury that the Widow Carberry was very wealthy; also that her only hopeful could wheedle her in to settling any sort of a bill he chose to contract, so that the mention of the sum of five hundred dollars was not anything extravagant for Percy.

"Oh! it wasn't that I doubted your word at all, Percy; don't think that," Chief Waller hastened to say; for like most men he was ready to bow down in front of the golden calf; and more than once Mrs. Carberry had been very generous to the force—when her house took fire and came near burning, but was saved, thanks to the energetic work of police and fire departments; and again, when a hired man tried to carry off some of her jewelry, but had been easily caught, and the plunder restored.

"Then what makes you act like that, I'd like to know?" demanded Percy, looking very much put out, as though he did not like to be treated with suspicion, especially when his old-time rivals, the Bird boys, were around.

"Why," the officer went on to say, "when you said that about your aeroplane being taken, it struck me all in a heap; because Frank here was just telling me that two men broke into his shop last night after eleven, and knocked things around, just because they failed to find his hydroplane in its bunk as usual. They wanted that machine, and wanted it so bad, that, as a last resort, they went over to your place, and confiscated your biplane."

It was Percy's turn now to look astonished. He even condescended to notice the presence of the two Bird boys, and surveyed them with interest.

"Is that a fact, Frank? Did somebody break into your place last night? I remember now that I did see you pottering about your craft up there somewhere about the Quackenboss place, but I'd forgotten it till the Chief mentioned that you didn't have it in the hangar. That's the time you were lucky. See what I got for having mine at home all snug and nice. It's been hooked clear as anything, and not a trace to tell who did the business."

"Hold on there, Percy," said the Chief, with a broad smile, "perhaps it isn't such a deep mystery after all."

"Tell me what you mean when you say that," demanded the boy, loftily, as though he resented the fact that anything should be kept from him a single second.

"Why, Frank and Andy found these things in their shop, left by the two men who tried to get their hydroplane; and the chances are ten to one the same parties went right straight over to your place and got yours as a second choice."

"I don't like the way you speak of my biplane, Chief, which cost ever so much more money than the contraption the Bird boys own," Percy remarked, sneeringly; "but never mind, tell me what these things stand for. An electric torch and—why those things look like black masks. Great Caesar! and the Bloomsbury bank was robbed last night, they told me when I was rushing around looking for you. See here, do you think the yeggs who did that neat job got away with my biplane?"

Percy was getting more excited than ever now. When he did, he seemed to just foam a little at the corners of his mouth, his eyes glittered, and his face turned red.

"There seems to be no doubt of it," replied the Chief, calmly, and yet with a stiffening of his figure, as though conscious of having already discovered a most promising clue, that could not but reflect credit on his astuteness as an officer of the law.

"They knew all about Frank's machine and mine too, then?" continued Percy, still grappling with the tremendous problem.

"Looks that way," the official went on to remark, "and makes me think more than ever that they must have a friend right here in Bloomsbury who put them wise to lots of things. Time'll tell that. But I don't suppose you found anything around your place like Frank did, to tell that some strangers had been there while you slept?"

"Not a blessed thing; though, to tell the honest truth, I didn't hang around long when I found my biplane was gone. It was the best machine I ever owned, and as you know I've had several, all told. And inside of three days I expected that the latest model of aluminum pontoons would be along, to turn it into a water as well as an air craft. Now chances are, I'll never see it again, because, like as not, nobody knows which way in creation they went."

"We happen to have a pointer about that same thing," Andy could not help saying, though he hardly liked the superior air of the other, not being able to overlook such things as easily as his cousin did.

"I hope, then, you'll give it to the Chief, Andy," the Carberry boy remarked, for the first time directly speaking to one of the cousins.

"Sure thing. We want to see the rascals copped just as much as anybody does. You see, Felix, he's the farm hand up at Mr. Quackenboss' place, and me, we thought it good policy to stay around, and keep an eye on our machine while it was lying overnight in that meadow. I had had a long watch of it, and was taking my turn at sleeping when just at daybreak Felix shook me, and said there was a queer noise up aloft that kind of scared him, and which he rather believed must come from some sort of air craft.

"Oh!" exclaimed Percy, looking intensely interested, of course; "go on, please."

"I jumped up, and sure enough I glimpsed a biplane passing over, and headed up the lake at a pretty good height, I thought it looked like your machine, but as I remarked to Frank later on, whoever steered it had a different way about him from your method. While I was wondering what took you out so early, and I could see there were two in the machine, a big flock of crows passed over, and I lost track of it.

"So, you see, Percy," broke in the eager Chief just at that point, "we've got a pretty good clue already about the direction the rascals took, who broke into the safe of the bank, and carried off a bagful of money, and valuable papers; and then followed that up by cribbing your biplane. It was north they went, up the lake, in fact; and that's the quarter we'll have to look for them. But let me tell you it's putting it pretty hard over on a police officer to make him try to track a stolen flying machine."

"But you can get in touch with every town to the north, and pick up pointers here and there!" Percy declared, excitedly. "Get back to town as fast as you can, Chief, and with a couple of your men I'll carry you wherever you want to go. In the meanwhile, you can leave orders for your men to do the wiring business; and whenever we strike a town we can ring up Headquarters over the 'phone, and learn what news they've managed to pick up."

Percy seemed to think that all he had to do was to tell the Chief what he wanted; but then his plan of campaign was really a good one, and the police officer was wise enough not to quarrel with his bread and butter; for the Widow Carberry was a large property owner in Bloomsbury.

"You just take the words out of my mouth seems like it," he remarked; "and that is the best plan we could carry out. I was just going to suggest to Frank and Andy here, that if they felt like taking a little spin off to the northward this fine morning, and discovered anything suspicious, they could get word to us, perhaps through the Bloomsbury Central, for we'll be apt to keep in touch with home."

Percy did not know whether to look pleased at this suggestion or not. It would be just like the everlasting luck of the Bird boys to make another remarkable success out of this thing, for they seemed to have a failing that way, while all the hard fortune came in his direction. That would give him a pain to be sure, for he was horribly envious of their local fame as successful aviators; but at the same time he hated to lose that beautiful biplane, which he had not owned very long, and which had taken his heart by storm.

So Percy finally compromised, as he frequently did. He even forced a grim smile to appear upon his face, though it did not deceive Frank in the least; and as for Andy, he never took the least stock in Percy Carberry's honesty. In his mind there was always a deep meaning underneath every action of the other.

"Why, sure I hope Frank will discover the thieves, and recover the stuff they've grabbed from the bank; also that he'll have the good luck to get back my biplane without its being badly wrecked. That reward is worth trying for, and I don't go back on my word."

All the same he knew very well that neither of the Bird boys could be forced to ever accept one penny from his hand, no matter what good Dame Fortune allowed them to do for him.

Andy was watching keenly when the Carberry boy walked back to his machine, and climbed into the steering seat. Frank, happening to look that way, saw his cousin's face lighted up as if in glee: and he even heard him chuckle. Perhaps Percy may have caught the same sound, for he turned his head after dropping down into his seat, and scowled darkly at Andy. There is nothing like a guilty conscience to bring about a self-betrayal; and somehow Percy seemed to know what the Bird boy was thinking about just then.

At any rate, he was an adept at the pilot wheel of a car, though inclined to be a reckless driver; just as he was also a daring air voyager, taking desperate chances that promised to bring him to grief one of these days.

Backing the car swiftly around, he sped away. Sandy Hollingshead, who had not once moved from his seat, or uttered a single word all the time, turned his head to look back; and Andy thought he too scowled darkly, as though stirred by unpleasant thoughts; but in another minute they had vanished around the bend far along the pike, and the Chief alone was seen, whipping up his nag, in the endeavor to get back as speedily as possible to Headquarters.

"Well, of all things, don't this just take the cake?" remarked Andy, when he and his cousin once more found themselves alone beside the motionless aeroplane, that nestled like a great bird on the grass close to the road.

"It certainly looks as though we might be in for a little more excitement," replied Frank; "but what seemed to make you chuckle so much, Andy? You must have noticed something that escaped my attention, because I was busy thinking of other things. Suppose you open up, and tell me?"

"I was tickled half to death to see how Percy tried to walk, as if nothing was the matter with him, when all the time he couldn't keep from limping; because, don't you see, one or several of those bird-shot Felix scattered around last night, must have stung him about the legs. That's why he scowled so at me, Frank!"

CHAPTER VII

THE AIR SCOUTS

Frank laughed a little, himself, when he heard his cousin say this.

"I give you credit for getting one on me there, Andy," he declared.

"Then you believe I hit the right nail on the head, do you, Frank?"

"Well," remarked the other, "come to think of it, Percy did have a little limp; and I guess he tried to hide it the best he could, for I remember seeing him wince several times. But how about Sandy, who never tried to get out of the car once, and didn't even open his lips to say a single word?"

"I bet you he got a double dose, and is pretty sore this morning." Andy went on. "You seemed to think it was kind of hard lines for Felix to give 'em a load when they were pretty far off, and just climbing over that fence; but it tickles me every time I think of it. Seemed like the whole bunch just fell over after he shot; and like as not each fellow got his share of the Number Eights somewhere in his legs. But how about this job the Chief asked us to engineer, Frank? Are we going to start off on that little spin up the lake; and d'ye guess we could get a pointer about where the two thieves have gone?"

"We might try, anyhow; no harm in that," was his cousin's reply, as he turned once more toward the hydroplane that lay near by.

"I remember we had great luck that other time, when we discovered that the men who broke into Leffingwell's place were hiding in that old cabin up in the woods. Perhaps the same story might be repeated, who knows? They call it the Bird boys' luck, Frank; but then, we work for all we get, and ought to have a little credit when we win out. If we made a bad job of things, the same people would be quick to say we didn't know our business. Shall we go back to the shop first?"

"That would be the only way," replied Frank. "If we're going to take on this dangerous job of looking up yeggmen who have broken into a bank, and looted it, why, it seems to me we ought to make a little preparation. Of course, about all we expect to do is to scout around, and see if we can pick up any information with the aid of our marine glasses. It's hardly to be expected that two boys would take the chance of trying to nab a couple of reckless thieves, who must be armed and desperate."

"But if the opening came, Frank, we wouldn't let it slip by, would we?" asked Andy, always willing to go to the limit, when temptation beckoned.

"Perhaps not," answered the other, smilingly; "but there's no use crossing a bridge till we come to it, so we won't bother any more about that. Get aboard, Andy, and we'll head for home again."

"Just think of all that's happened since we had that little accident yesterday afternoon, up near the Quackenboss place?" Andy went on to say, as he complied with his cousin's request, and settled himself in his seat, leaving the piloting of the machine to Frank.

"There has been quite a little run of excitement, that's a fact," mused the other; "first the accident, and our great good luck in making a landing without breaking a thing, including our precious necks."

"Then the discovery of Percy and Sandy looking at the hydroplane lying there, and hurrying away as if they had already laid a plan to come back and pay a night visit, if they failed to see us get home by daylight," Andy went on to add.

"Events followed thick and fast after that, Andy—the coming of the four fellows, with their faces hidden; their repulse at the hands of yourself and the friendly Felix; then the robbery of the bank; the breaking into our shop by men who left their cards behind in the shape of these burglar tools; the meeting of the Chief on the road, and the news he gave us; and last of all the coming of Percy with the startling news that his biplane had been stolen!"

"Yes, but don't forget my seeing it sailing over just at early dawn," remarked the other, as Frank stooped forward for a last look around, before starting up the powerful little Kinkaid engine. "Because that promises to play quite a figure in the pursuit of the smart thieves; though they may be fifty miles away from here by now, if they know how to handle that fine biplane right."

"Hold tight; we're off!" warned Frank, as he applied the power; for the new engine was of course a self-starter, and could be operated from his seat with almost as much ease as might be shown in using electricity, and pressing the button.

The hydroplane ran easily along the ground, for the bicycle wheels were always kept in first class condition; and as the speed kept on increasing Frank soon uptilted the plane, and like a great bird rising from the ground, with a graceful sweep the flying machine took to the air.

Long practice had made the Bird boys familiar with every movement connected with the actions of an aeroplane, but at the same time they tried to be always on their guard against being incautious. That is the trouble with most aviators; they grow so familiar with danger that they forget the terrible risk that always hangs over the head of every one who soars aloft in his frail airship; and then, when finally something happens after they have become too reckless, they never get another chance.

Sweeping along not more than three hundred feet above the ground, the boys were home in almost no time. They could see the car containing Percy Carberry, and his crony, Sandy, just vanishing among the houses of Bloomsbury; and the Chief, about half-way there, waved his hat at them as they sped past him.

Then the aeroplane dropped lightly down close to the hangar back of the Bird home, where Andy and his father, the professor, lived, together with old Colonel Whympers, the veteran who used crutches or a cane on account of his rheumatism, brought on, he always declared, not by age, oh! no, but the wounds he received many years ago, when he was fighting for his country in the great civil war.

He was sitting there on a pile of lumber waiting for them, a quaint old fellow, who was greatly beloved by both cousins; and who believed firmly that some fine day Andy Bird was bound to even eclipse the fame which his father had gained in the field of science and aviation.

It happened that the professor was away at the time delivering a series of lectures before some body of scientists in a distant city. And whenever the boys were in their shop the old veteran was in the habit of coming around, to see what new and wonderful things engaged their attention, as well as chatting with them. And he was as welcome as the sun in May.

Of course, just then he was bristling with questions as a hedgehog would be with sharp-pointed quills. And knowing the Colonel of old, Frank and Andy lost no time in telling him all that had happened to them, from the time of their little accident, down to when they heard the latest news from Percy Carberry.

"And I warrant now," remarked Colonel Whimpers, as soon as the tale was finished, "that you two boys get the first clew to where the robbers are hiding. Didn't you beat the wonderful Chief out before, and doesn't history have a habit of repeating itself? Oh; if only I was ten years younger, how I'd love to be along, when all these glorious things are happening. I hate to think I'm put by on the shelf and never can be any good again."

That was the old man's only fault; he was forever complaining because his day for indulging in exciting scenes had passed; but any one who knew the half that he had passed through, would think the colonel had no reason to say anything; and that it was only right that someone else had a show.

They soon soothed him, however, and long practice had made Andy particularly apt at this sort of thing.

"Here come Elephant and Larry, on the run," remarked Frank, a little while later; "I wonder if they saw us come home, and whether they can have picked up any additional news connected with the bank robbery, that we ought know."

"Well, it might pay us to hold up a little, and see," added Andy.

"Yes, since we're in no great hurry, and the day is long," Frank remarked.

The two boys came up panting for breath. Larry had evidently set the pace, and it was a matter of the smaller lad keeping with him, or else being left behind, something Elephant never liked to have happen; so that he was unable to say even a single word for a full minute after arriving alongside the hangar.

"Tell us, have they learned anything new since the Chief started off?" asked Frank, as usual right to the point; and in this way cutting off the myriad of questions which he knew both the newcomers were primed to ask.

"Why, yes," gasped Larry, while Elephant nodded his head as if to say he agreed to all that was said, "after Percy came bustling around, asking for the Chief, and telling how somebody had busted into his place, and run off with his biplane in the night, they got to talking it over, and wondering if it could have been the robbers, and if one of 'em knew how to handle such things. So they called up the city, and asked questions. In that way they learned that there was a yegg who had been suspected of having been connected with several other jobs, though they never could just put the kibosh on him, and his name is Casper Blue, and one time he used to be an actor, and then became a pretty well-known flier, but in an accident he broke his arm, and had to give up his business. He was always a crooked sort of feller, and after that just boozed around, joined in with hobo gangs, and they believe touched up a few jobs himself. There, that's all we know; and now, what you been doing?"

"Too long a story to tell just now," declared Frank. "The colonel knows, and perhaps he'll amuse you after we've gone."

"Oh! say, are you meanin' to take after them fellers that busted the bank safe, and then got away with Percy's biplane?" asked Elephant eagerly; "don't I wish though I could just hang on behind, and be in the swim for once. You two seem to have about all the fun there is going, hang the luck, say I?"

"Well, you'd better not try it, that's what!" said Andy, shaking his head threateningly at the bare suggestion of having Elephant aboard when they made a start.

"I think we've got everything now, Andy," remarked Frank, anxious to be off.

"Hope you're taking guns along, because if you do run across them hobo fellers you'll be apt to need them right bad," Larry went on to say, also looking downcast at having to miss all the sport simply because Nature had never intended him for an aviator, as he was inclined to get dizzy when looking down from any height.

"Oh! Frank's provided for that, and besides, we don't really expect to round the thieves up, just find out if they've dropped down anywhere inside of thirty miles to the north of Bloomsbury. Shall I get aboard, Frank?"

"Yes; and after we're off, Larry, will you and Elephant do me the favor to step around to my house, and tell my folks that the Bird boys have hired out as scouts to Chief Waller? Tell dad that we'll be mighty careful, and for mother not to worry about us. You know I always call Aunt Laura mother, because she's been that ever since my own died years ago. Will you do that, boys?" and Frank sitting there ready to start, turned a smiling face upon his two friends. Even as they promised, the aeroplane started off, and a minute later soared up in the air, like a bird rejoicing at its freedom for leaving the earth behind.

CHAPTER VIII

JUST BELOW THE CLOUDS

"Good luck to you, boys!" came floating up from the ground, above the buzzing of the busy little Kinkaid motor; and looking down, they could see Larry, Elephant, yes, and the old veteran also, carrying on excitedly, as they swung their hats around.

"Who're you waving your handkerchief to, Frank; does your best girl keep her eyes on the skies all the day long, looking to see you come around?" demanded Andy, humorously.

"Yes, that's my best girl, as sure as you live; and she's standing there on the porch of our house right now, waving to me—Aunt Laura, who thinks just as much of me as any mother could. But Andy, neither of us said anything when Larry told about that hobo aviator named Casper Blue; yet he answered the description the bank watchman gave of the smaller man who had a stiff arm."

"Oh, I noticed that, all right, even if I didn't look your way," returned Andy, promptly. "It sort of clinched the nail we drove through didn't it, Frank?"

"Seems like it," the other went on to remark. "And the chances are ten to one, we've got the story down fine right now, know who one of the robbers was, why they wanted to steal an aeroplane to make their get-away in, and all that. But there are a few things we don't know, that'd throw a little more light on the affair."

"As what?" queried his cousin.

"Well, for one thing, the Chief seemed to think the thieves might have had inside information, they seemed to know so much about things connected with the bank, our having an aeroplane, where we lived, what our habits were, and then about Percy's biplane in the bargain. Now, that's something serious; if there's a man in Bloomsbury who's in league with such rascals he'll be apt to help them out again later on if they get away with this job; and he ought to be found out."

"Whew! looks like we've got a big job on our hands if we hope to do all that sort of thing," commented Andy, with a whistle to indicate his feelings.

"Nobody said we even think of trying," laughed Frank, as he stopped mounting upward in spirals, and headed away toward the north.

It was a glorious view that they had now spread out beneath and around them. Neither of the Bird boys ever tired of such wonderful sights; and although by now it had become an old story, they enjoyed it as much as ever, even if their former sensation of awe had given way to one of familiarity.

They could see the entire outlines of beautiful Lake Sunrise, with its many coves, and points jutting out, the water glistening in the sunlight, as the morning breeze fanned it gently.

Why, yes, there was the little lake steamboat called the Mermaid, passing along the northern border of the lake, on the way between the town of Cranford, on the shore opposite Bloomsbury, and headed toward a small lumbering camp far up the left bank, possibly to deliver supplies, after which she would point her nose down toward the home town, which was of more importance than any other station on Lake Sunrise.

The boys did look back, dear though the scenes around home must ever be for them. It was characteristic of these lads that once they put their shoulder to the wheel, or in other words, their hand to the plow, they would not allow themselves to be discouraged by thoughts of the home ties. That accounted for much of the success that had been their portion in the past. They could for the time being forget that there was any such place as home; and in this way they avoided the weakness that such thoughts are apt to bring along in their train.

Forward their way lay, toward those forbidding wilds far to the north, where few towns could be found, and pretty much all the country was a vast wilderness, filled with picturesque forests, wild swamps, and rugged hills.

It was just the country where desperate law breakers would choose as a hiding-place, after they had committed some crime, and expected a warm pursuit. Ordinary methods would never find them, save through a mere chance; but when one can copy the eagle, and mount to dizzy heights, with a pair of powerful glasses he can see almost everything that is going on for miles and miles around, provided he has a skilled companion along to manage the aeroplane or balloon.

And that is destined to be the greatest value of these winged messengers in future years, since it has been proven that they are not so very dangerous after all in the line of dropping explosives upon battleships or fortified places.

"Somewhere up yonder, Frank, they are probably hiding, and feeling perfectly safe from pursuit," ventured Andy, who was sweeping the marine glasses around and examining the country ahead with more than common interest.

"Look how Old Thunder-top stands out today!" remarked Frank, turning for just an instant to glance upward toward the left, where the high mountain towered, its heavily wooded sides looking as gloomy as ever, and the white cliffs that made the summit inaccessible to human feet, appearing almost dazzling in the glittering light of the undimmed morning sun.

"And say, there's our old friends, the eagles that had a nest up there, and gave me such a warm time when we first reached the top." Andy cried, as he focused his glasses on a sweeping pair of huge birds that were heading their way, as if meaning to investigate, and find out what manner of rival this could be, invading their native element.

"They know too much to bother with an aeroplane by now!" declared Frank, laughing again. "Why I'm thinking those birds have hardly grown new feathers in place of the lot they lost that time they fought us so savagely."

The memory appeared to amuse his cousin also, for he could be heard laughing heartily, even above the purr of the now steadily going motor that sent the propellers whizzing around so rapidly; for there was one fore and aft, as is the case with all biplanes, the engine being behind the pilot and his companion.

"Tell me if you can remember, was that other aeroplane headed straight up the lake the last you saw it in the early morning light?" Frank asked.

"That's right, Frank; but then I couldn't say just how long they kept along that same course. When those hundreds of old crows came sailing along on the wind, cawing to beat the band, and going every-which-way, I lost sight of the biplane. After that it would have to be just guess work."

"But we've got a good pointer to start with," insisted Frank. "They wouldn't be so apt to head toward the south, east or west, because in those directions there are plenty of towns and villages, and these could report seeing a strange biplane passing over, so giving the police a clue. No, chances are ten to one they kept right on toward the north. And there's where we've got to do all our searching today. We can just comb the whole district over, and anything that looks like the stolen aeroplane is sure to catch our attention from this height, don't you think so, Andy?"

"I reckon it will, Frank; but the only thing bothers me is that things may have worked all right with the rascals, and by now they're away off, so far distant that we'll never in the wide world get in touch with them, the more the pity."

"Well, it's never been a habit of ours to own up beaten till we've done everything under the sun to win out. And Andy, we've only started as yet. The field is before us, you know, with a whole day's supply of gas to push us on, if we want to keep going. So I'm not asking any favors, and expect to do just my level best to find out where the bank robbers have gone."

"And if we hunt around a whole lot without getting tabs on the pair, why, we can drop down somewhere in a town, and get in touch with Bloomsbury Headquarters. The Chief as much as promised that he'd leave word there to put us wise to anything that had been learned by way of the telephone, from other places. And given a clue in that way, we might take a fresh spurt, you know."

"Just so, Andy," agreed the other, bending his head to watch how some part of the machinery was doing its duty; for that is always the weak link in modern aviation, nearly everything depending on the engine fulfilling its part perfectly.

Andy continued to make use of the pair of glasses that magnified objects in the far distance so wonderfully that a man could have been recognized easily a mile away, and perhaps much further, if the air were real clear.

Now and then he turned them to the right. The beautiful lake always attracted him very much like a magnet would, whenever he had a chance to look out over its glistening bosom.

And there was the little steamer, just as Frank had said; why, he could even distinguish Todd Pemberton up in the pilothouse, grasping his wheel and guiding his charge among the shoals that were charted in the northern end of the lake as dangerous, that is, for green hands at the tiller or wheel of a boat propelled by sails, steam or gasolene.

They were moving in a line that would carry them up along the shore, and consequently every minute they drew nearer the small lake steamer that was heading toward them.

Passengers could be seen on its deck, and possibly every eye was glued just at that particular moment on the aeroplane that was buzzing go steadily northward; perhaps it might have been the first time some of these people had ever seen such an interesting object; but in the region around Bloomsbury it was by now a common sight, with such enterprising young air pilots as the Bird boys and Percy Carberry in the field almost every decent day.

All at once Frank was heard to utter an exclamation.

"Turn your glasses straight ahead, and see what that can be fluttering among the bushes at Norton's Point, Andy!" he called out hastily.

When the other had swung around, and covered the region spoken of, he quickly gave the desired information.

"Somebody seems to be shaking a handkerchief or something else white," he observed. "And it don't look like just waving at the steamer either, for they do it after a system, as we would signal with wigwag flags. There, I counted seven times he did it; then comes a halt, and one, two, three times, another halt; and once more he starts in, this time three, four, five, and then stops. Now, what do you suppose the fellow means by that, and who can he be waving to, Frank?"

"You'd expect it might be some one out on the lake; can you see any small boat in sight, Andy; or any one waving back from another point?"

"Not a thing, as far as I can see," replied the boy with the marine glasses.

"Suppose you try the steamer, then," suggested Frank, meaningly.

Immediately Andy gave an exclamation of astonishment.

"I see a signal moving, Frank, and it seems to be copying the one on shore," he hastened to remark, excitedly.

"Where does it come from, the passengers that I saw pushing up against the rail, and staring at us; are any of them interested, do you think?" continued Frank, who just then could not turn his head to look, but must depend on his chum.

"Well, no," answered Andy, "it seems to come from the pilothouse, and must be Todd Pemberton, himself."

CHAPTER IX

THE PILOT OF THE MERMAID

"So, it's Todd Pemberton, is it?" remarked Frank, "I think it'll pay us to slow down a little, and look into this white rag-waving business."

"Goodness gracious! you can't be thinking that Todd is in touch with the bank robbers, can you, Frank?" Andy exclaimed, astounded, apparently, at the very thought of such a thing.

"Oh! I'm not up to that point of saying anything—yet. But all the same it's what I call interesting, you know," the other replied; and from this Andy could easily guess that while Frank might have notions about the matter, he did not care to commit himself so early in the game.

"Yes, that's so," Andy replied, still having his eyes glued to the binoculars.

"What's doing now?" continued Frank.

"Nothing that I c'n see," replied the other.

"No more white handkerchiefs waving around the point, eh, Andy?"

"Not a blessed thing; and Todd's quit too. Guess they've come to some sort of an understanding. Wish I knew what seven, three, five meant; something pretty interesting, I'll be bound." Andy went on to mutter, half to himself.

"Well, we can only guess, and that's the extent of it," Frank was saying, in a rather serious tone, as though he believed there might be more in connection with the little affair than a mere exchange of civilities.

"How about Todd Pemberton, Frank?" asked the boy with the glasses.

"Well, you know him as well as I do, perhaps better," returned his cousin.

"I mean, wasn't there once something against him? I know, Frank, that my guardian signed a paper about getting Todd his position with the steamboat company this last spring; they always get him to sign everything going, he's so good-natured and what you call an Easy Mark."

"Yes, they came to my father too, and he put his name down, I remember. As near as I can say, it was a petition to ask the company to give Todd the position of pilot; and stated the belief of all those who signed that he would make good. He used to be a pilot on Lake Sunrise, and before that on one of the Great Lakes."

"But, Frank, why the petition, if he was able to fill the place you'd think all he had to do was to make application, and then jump in?"

"Well, it seemed to be pretty generally known about Bloomsbury that Todd had not always been as straight as he is today; and lots of people believed he would never hold his place a week; but he's had it all summer now, and seems to be giving satisfaction, all right," Frank went on to say.

"But there was a past, you mean; Todd had gone the pace, and used to drink and gamble, I suppose. Perhaps, now, he even used to herd with a tough set. How about that, Frank?"

"It's so all right. Todd got down pretty low, and was even a hobo, I heard, before he took a brace, and came back to Bloomsbury to make a man of himself again."

"Gee! I'm real sorry to hear that," Andy muttered.

"What? That he reformed?" demanded the cousin, in pretended surprise.

"Shucks! no; but about his having been a tramp; because, don't you see, Frank, it makes things look black for Todd. Remember, don't you, about what the Chief said when he spoke of the yeggs knowing so much about things, that he thought they must have had inside information; and that somebody familiar with Bloomsbury ways helped them figure it all out. Looks bad for Todd, that's what, Frank."

To hear Andy talk you would think that the party in question must have been a personal friend, at least, when, in truth, he only knew Todd Pemberton to speak to, as he did a thousand other people in and around the home town.

"By that you mean you're afraid he's fallen in with some old companions in crime and been tempted, or forced to join them in this raid on the bank?" was the way Frank put the matter direct.

"You've covered what I do believe, as sure as my name's Andy Bird."

"Well, let me say that I think the same way you do," Frank went on to remark.

"Good!" cried Andy, in a delighted tone. "Sometimes we agree, and again we have different minds; but in this case it looks like we might be on the same raft."

"Take another good squint at the point, Andy, and see if you can pick up that man again, the fellow who was doing all that tall Wigwagging."

"I'm looking, Frank."

"What d'ye see there now?" the other continued.

"Nothing—that is, there are stones, and moss, and trees, and perhaps birds flying around this way and that; but never the first sign of a human being can I discover anywhere, Frank."

"Still, we know there's one man there at least, perhaps a pair of them hiding somewhere around that desolate place. Why, Norton's Point is, I guess, about the meanest and loneliest place of all the Disston Swamp lumber company. Nobody hardly ever goes there except to shoot snipe and woodcock in the fall, and yet we happen to know there's one person hiding out there, and that he knows Todd Pemberton, for they've been exchanging signals through the wigwag code."

"Looks suspicious, Frank, don't you think?"

"Looks like it might pay to investigate a little closer, Andy."

They were by this time passing over the identical strip of country where Andy had watched the signal waving. By looking almost directly down, he could see between the tall trees as only an aviator ever has a chance of doing.

"You know what I'm hoping to discover, Frank?" he remarked as he continued to scan every part that was at all exposed by openings among the trees.

"Percy's lost biplane, I take it," came the prompt reply.

"Yes, because they couldn't very well have landed without a certain amount of open space. We know how hard it is to drop into a hole, and worse still to climb up out of one. Didn't we have the toughest of times down there in that South American forest finding open spots where we could land with some chance of ever getting out again, without cutting trees down that were as big around as a young house?"

"But I don't hear you shouting out that you've made any sort of discovery, up to now, Andy?"

"Well, no, for a fact I haven't. But Frank, I wish you could take the glass and let me hold the wheel for a minute."

"You can tell me just as well, I think," replied the other.

"It's about the sandy beach in front of the point," remarked Andy.

"What ails it then?" Frank inquired, seeing his cousin hesitate.

"Why," Andy went on to say, "you know how powerful this glass is, and how it shows up the smallest of things when the sun is just right? It's doing that now. I can look down on the sand spit at the point; and for a lonely spot where hardly a man ever comes from November to June, it looks pretty well trampled up to me."

"Trampled by men or animals?" the pilot inquired.

"I think by two-legged animals," answered the one who held the powerful lenses to his young eyes. "And it struck me that perhaps the biplane came down right there early this morning. It was headed this way when I saw it, and not so very high up; though that flock of crazy crows knocked me out of watching it for some times."

"Do you mean it fell there; that they had an accident of some kind, Andy?"

"Might be that; and then, again, perhaps they dropped down on purpose; p'raps they mean to have another warm session around Bloomsbury before skipping out of this section for good. With the aeroplane to make a quick get-away, they might think of some rich haul they want to gather in. Am I away off in my guess, Frank, or do you kind of lean the same way?"

"I think you are getting pretty close to the truth, Andy, and that's a fact," replied the other. "But it would clinch it if you could only glimpse the biplane hidden away somewhere down there under the brush or the trees."

"That's what I've been hoping for," returned Andy, a little fretfully, "but so far without meeting any success that you could notice. But what ought we to do about it, Frank?"

"Go on, and take a wide sweep around," came the steady reply. "Perhaps we might run across another leading clue, and then this one would look foolish. We'd be sorry then, that we thought so bad of Todd. Perhaps, after all, he was only making signals to one of the men connected with the logging camp, up on the Point for something or other."

He allowed the motor to work at the reduced speed that it had been carrying on ever since quitting the home field, where the workshop and the hangar stood. Andy still continued to use the glasses, as though he had not quite given up all hope of making some sort of discovery.

Once, however, they had left the northern end of the lovely lake behind them for good, and only the forest lay below, Frank quickened matters somewhat. Truth to tell, he hardly knew what to think, and whether what they had witnessed could really have any bearing on the solution of the puzzle or not.

Certainly if the hunt was only kept up in automobiles, that required fairly decent roads to allow of their getting along, there was not much chance of the authorities ever discovering the concealed hobo thieves; for they could not get within a mile of the shore up there at Norton's Point by such methods. The only way it could be reached was by boat; or possibly through the means of an aeroplane, such as the Bird boys were now using. Few places but could be spied upon, when one had the means for passing over the most inaccessible thickets and rocky hills.

After a time they had gone many miles. Occasionally a small hamlet was seen below; and then would come once more the woods that extended over such a large space of territory in this part of the country. This was generally because of the swampy nature of the ground, which prevented farming operations being carried on, while the difficulty of getting the logs out of the bogs had deterred lumbering thus far.

Andy had done his part of the work faithfully. He had scoured the territory over which they passed, and never did a break occur, however small, but he clapped his eyes upon it, and examined the open space thoroughly.

"There's Rockford ahead, and we've passed over the whole stretch of swamp and forest. Suppose, now, we dropped down on the commons, and get Bloomsbury on the long distance phone; perhaps they might have some news they could give us," and as Andy at once agreed to the proposal, for he was thirsty anyhow, and wanted a drink of soda water the worst kind, Frank began to descend gracefully.

They had about half the population of the place gaping at them as they finally landed on the big green. Frank asked his cousin to stay by the machine while he sought police headquarters, and asked to get in touch with the home town.

He had no sooner made the connection, and heard some one answer him after he told who he was, when there was sent along the wire some information that rather gave Frank a shock, because of its nature, and the fact that it seemed to fully dispose of the theory he and his cousin had already formed.

CHAPTER X

HEARD OVER THE WIRE

Luckily the center of interest remained around the odd looking aeroplane with the metal pontoons underneath its body, so that Frank was allowed to walk away almost unnoticed, when he had secured the important information he inquired for, and which was leading him to the drug store nearest the town green.

True, an aviator had landed in Rockford on one or two occasions, for some reason or other, in times past. Since the Bird boys could not remember having done so, possibly it may have been Percy Carberry, anxious to enjoy the stares of the good people, and pose as a great fellow.

But this was a type of air machine with which none of them were familiar; and as so much space was being taken up even in the local papers with the accounts of the wonderful doings of daring navigators of the upper currents, it was only natural that some bright boy should speedily guess what manner of craft the chance visitor to Rockford must be.

"Hey! that's a hyderplane, mister, ain't it?" demanded one sharp-eyed chap, after he had glimpsed the construction of the aluminum pontoons that were just kept from contact with the ground by the bicycle wheels.

"Have you ever seen one before?" asked Andy, desirous of keeping up friendly relations with the crowd, for he knew how important that might prove, since, as yet, no man wearing a blue uniform had put in an appearance; and should any hoodlum choose to play "rough house," or try to be too familiar with the apparatus, there was always a chance that some damage might be done.

"No, I ain't, but I seen a picture of that 'ere Coffyn feller, a-flyin' down on the Hudson river nigh New York; and she looked a heap like this here shebang," came the quick response.

"Well, you guessed right that time, for that is what it is called, a hydroplane; because it can be navigated on the water as well as in the air. And if you'll please stand back, so as not to bother with anything, because the least handling may put the whole machine out of tune, I'll be glad to tell you something about how we manage to use it as a boat."

Andy knew how to manage, and he exerted himself to entertain the crowd while Frank was absent, keeping their interest aroused by little stories of things that had happened to birdmen in recent times, and which were of course well known to him, from the fact that both the cousins kept in close touch with all that went on in the world of aviation.

All the while Andy was keeping one anxious eye out for the sign of a blue uniform and brass buttons, while new additions kept arriving constantly to swell the eager crowd gathered on the park green.

In the end he was vastly relieved to discover a policeman hurrying up, looking as serious as though he expected to discover a fight, or two youngsters matching pet roosters, to the delight of the gathered host; for since the flying machine lay on the ground it was mostly concealed from his view; and he would never have known what it was anyway.

Of course, when he arrived on the scene and took command Andy quickly gained his favor by a little subtle flattery; and after that felt that he was, as he himself expressed it, "on Easy Street."

Meanwhile Frank had proceeded direct to the drugstore on the corner, about two blocks away from the end of the green, where they had told him he could talk over the long distance phone with Bloomsbury.

He was pleased to find that they had a regular booth in the store; for he knew of numerous cases where the phone simply stood on a little stand, and everybody could hear what the subject of the talk might be, especially one side of it.

Once closeted in the booth he hastened to ask for connection with Police Headquarters at Bloomsbury. There was some little delay, as though these long distance calls might be of rare occurrence in the local Central; but finally he received notice that connection had been made, and he was at liberty to start his message.

"Hello! this Bloomsbury?" Frank asked first of all in a cautious way.

"Yes," came the reply, distinctly enough.

"And is this Police Headquarters?"

"Yes."

"This is Frank Bird speaking and we are over in Rockford; get that?" Frank continued.

"Yes," again came the reply from the party at the other end.

"Chief Waller asked us before we left Bloomsbury to keep in touch with Headquarters, and that you would supply us with any new information that might come to hand while we scoured the country overhead, looking for signs of the men who robbed the Bloomsbury bank last night, and escaped in Percy Carberry's biplane. Who is this I am talking to, please?"

"Officer Green, Frank."

"Oh! is that you, Joe; I didn't recognize your voice over the wire," Frank went on to say. "You heard what the Chief said about giving us the latest news, didn't you, Joe?"

"I certain did, Frank," answered the man at the other end of the wire.

"We've covered quite a large territory up to now, and think we've run across a clue; but we want to make sure before putting the bloodhounds of the law on the scent. Get that?"

Frank was wise to the fact that Officer Green took himself and his position on the local police force very seriously. True, he had never done anything very great, to distinguish himself, beyond once stopping a runaway horse that some people said was too decrepit to have gone twenty paces further; and rescuing a little pet dog that had fallen into the lake from a wharf; but then he believed in himself; and read up all the thrilling stories of police achievements that were published in the New York papers, satisfied that sooner or later the day was bound to come when he would be able to prove himself a grand hero.

And that was just why artful Frank used that phrase "bloodhounds of the law," for he knew that it would cause Joe Green to puff up with pride, and feel more kindly disposed than ever toward the speaker.

He gauged matters exactly right, too, it seemed; for when the police officer spoke again it was with additional eagerness.

"Good for you, Frank; all Bloomsbury expects the Bird boys to do the old town proud again. Many the time have you done it in the past, we all know. And when you feel dead sure that you've got track of the desprit villains who looted our town bank, all you have to do is to give the police the signal, and they'll throw a drag-net around the hang-out of the yeggs. That's what we're here for; that's what we draw our salaries for; to protect the citizens of Bloomsbury against danger by fire, flood, robbers and the like."

Frank knew only too well how Officer Green liked to talk, especially when once started on the subject of his exalted office; and accordingly he thought it time to cut him short, before he could get launched on the sea of police duties.

"Tell me, have you learned anything new since we left?" he asked.

"Why, yes, we've just had a man in here, who had heard about the robbery, and that it was suspected the thieves had escaped by means of the biplane belonging to the Carberry boy. He thought as how we might be glad to know that he'd sighted a flying machine just after daybreak."

"Why, yes, that ought to be an important piece of news," remarked Frank, wondering whether it would corroborate that which the farm hand, Felix Boggs, had already contributed to the fund of knowledge concerning the movements of the fleeing yeggmen.

"I thought it was; and I'm only waiting right now to forward it to the Chief, as soon as he calls me on the wire from Hazenhurst, or some other place where he's apt to turn Up," came over the wire from the home town.

"Don't cut me off, yet, Central!" called out Frank, hastily, as he thought he detected an uneasy movement, which was doubtless a sigh given by the girl, who possibly had her ear to the wire, drinking in what was being said: "I'm not near done talking yet. Hello! Joe!"

"Yes, I'm here, Frank; what more do you want to ask me?" came from miles away; and in imagination he could see Officer Green crouched at the telephone stand, as he remembered it at Police Headquarters in Bloomsbury, feeling the importance of his relations with the public as a genuine guardian of the peace.

"Why, it's of considerable importance to us to know in which direction the aeroplane was going at the time this party sighted it," Frank went on to say, "and I hope he told you that."

"Which he did without my asking," replied Officer Green, quickly, "though you may be sure I would have done the same before letting him leave, because I was on to the fact that it would be a pretty good pointer."

"Oh! he thought of it himself, did he?" the young aviator shot back, "well, that was pretty bright of him, and shows that he was a fellow to take notice. And now, please tell me what he said about the direction in which the biplane was headed, at the last instant he could see it far away in the distance."

"Exactly southwest, Frank!"

This gave Frank a sudden jar, because it upset the theories he and Andy had been forming concerning the escaping bank robbers. They had believed the two men had gone almost directly north!

"Southwest, you say, Joe?" he asked, wishing to make assurance doubly sure.

"He said exactly southwest; and as he kept repeating that word a number of times there isn't a bit of chance that I'd get it mixed. You can depend on it, Frank, and if you're away up at Rockford, seems to me you'll have to make a big change of base right soon, if you want to get in touch with them raskils."

Frank's mind was in somewhat of a whirl. He wondered whether the farm hand, Felix Boggs, could have been mistaken in what he had said; though Andy, too, had seen the biplane, and noted the direction of its flight. But perhaps this farmer, or whoever he might turn out to be, had discovered the fugitive flying machine at a much later time, after the two men had changed the course of their flight.

"I suppose you might as well tell me who the party was from whom you got your news, Joe," he remarked; though without any particular object in view, since he could hardly expect to hunt the other up, and ask more questions.

And then came the answer, that gave Frank quite a thrill, as he grasped the peculiar significance of it all.

"Why, you know him all right, Frank," said Officer Green, glibly, "he's the pilot of the little lake steamer, and his name's Todd Pemberton!"

CHAPTER XI

COMPARING NOTES

"He must have hurried up to Headquarters, then, as soon as he landed, because we saw the Mermaid crossing the northern end of the lake, bound for the lumber camp, before heading for Bloomsbury. How about it, Joe?" Frank went on to ask, as soon as he had recovered from his surprise after hearing that particular name mentioned.

"Said he heard about the robbery," came over the wire in Officer Green's ponderous tones; "and the fact of the raskils skipping out with the Carberry boy's biplane, as soon as he put foot ashore; and thinking that the police might like to know what he had seen, he just ran all the way here."

"Which I take it was mighty thoughtful of Todd," declared Frank, drily; but if he spoke sarcastically the fact was not known to the man at the other end.

"I told him so, and complimented him on his zeal in assisting the course of justice," the other continued, "which was all the more remarkable, you know, Frank, because, to tell the truth, Todd himself was once a bad egg, until he reformed, and got his present job. It does him great credit, sure it does."

"He went away after letting you know that if you hoped to capture the thieves you'd have to chase southwest, and not north, didn't he, Joe?"

"Oh! yes, about ten minutes ago, I reckon. But I assured him that if we did succeed in capturing the rogues he would not be forgotten in the division of the reward that was sure to be offered by the bank for the recovery of the money and securities that were taken, not to speak of the five hundred young Carberry has said he would pay for the recovery of his biplane and the arrest of the thieves."

"That was nice of you, Joe; but only what might be expected because your heart is as big as a bushel basket," Frank went on to say, "and when you told Todd that, how did he take it?"

"Why, he just chuckled, and looked at me kind of funny, and said he never hoped to take any of the hard-earned reward money that the police were justly entitled to because of their activities," replied the other.

"It's plain to be seen that Todd is a generous fellow. But I'm obliged to you, Joe, for giving me this information, because, you see, we've now got some foundation to build on. Goodbye, Joe!"

With that Frank rang off. He knew that he might chat with the gossipy police officer in Bloomsbury for at least fifteen minutes, but what was the use, when he already knew all the other had to tell?

And the news that had come over the wire was of considerable importance, too. He smiled as he hurried out of the drugstore, not even waiting to quench his thirst at the soda fountain, though a short time before he, as well as Andy, had complained of feeling so exceedingly dry; but then, all that was now forgotten in this excitement connected with the latest development in the robbery case.

It was back to the village green, now, with Frank.

The crowd was greater than ever, and he quickly saw there would be no opportunity for any communication between himself and his cousin until they had left for the upper realms, where, surrounded only by silence, they could converse while the busy motor hummed and the aeroplane headed as they willed, either high above the hills, or skirting the tops of the forest trees.

Accordingly, Frank addressed himself to the arduous task of getting away without any mishap. He, as well as Andy, had long since learned that it is the part of wisdom to gain the good will of a curious crowd. In that manner many friends are raised up, who are only too willing to lend a helping hand.

He quickly selected half a dozen fellows who looked as though they might be of more than ordinary importance among the boys of Rock-ford. These he particularly picked out, and asked them to assist the police officer to keep the crowd back until they could get a good start, at the same time explaining that a clear passage would have to be made ahead, and that anyone getting in the way might not only be seriously injured, but wreck the machine as well.

Proud to have been thus honored, the six boys proceeded to push back the gaping crowd and when Frank gave the word, also assisted in starting the hydroplane on its way.

A salvo of loud cheers rang out when they started, and this burst into a furious chorus as the well balanced aeroplane presently left the ground to start upward into the air.

"I'm glad that's over with," said Andy, when they were safely off the ground, and the shouts of Rockford's enthusiastic population began to grow fainter in the distance.

"Same here," echoed Frank, "you never know what will happen when a crowd is pushing all around you, every fellow eager to just say he had hold of a flying machine. There's always one or two of the lot ready to hang on and risk their lives just to see how it feels to be carried up on an aeroplane. They're the kind I'm most afraid of."

"Well, did you get Police Headquarters in Bloomsbury, Frank?"

"No trouble about that; and our old friend, Officer Green, was in charge during the absence of the Chief," the other Bird boy answered.

"Anything new developed since we left?" asked Andy.

"Just one thing, and Joe thought it meant a whole lot," Frank went on to say.

"Which was what?" inquired the other.

"A man came hurrying in and told how he had seen a flying machine containing two parties just after daybreak, and making directly toward the southwest, Andy. What do you think of that now for news?"

His cousin gave a whistle.

"Whew! important, if true!" he vouchsafed, tersely.

"That sounds as if you had some trouble believing it?" chuckled Frank.

"Well, considering what I saw myself, I'd have to know the name of this party first, before I'd believe anything he said," Andy went on.

"Oh! You know him, alright; fact is, we were speaking of the same not a great while back," Frank observed, quietly.

"Don't make me start in guessing, Frank, because we've been talking of a dozen people; but tell me right out who it is," Andy pleaded.

"The pilot of the Mermaid, Andy!"

"Gee! Do you mean Todd Pemberton?" exclaimed the other.

"Just him and no one else. Why, he was that anxious to let the police know he had seen an aeroplane steering away straight into the southwest early this morning, that as soon as he warped his boat to the wharf, Todd, like a public-spirited citizen, hiked away for Headquarters as fast as he could run, hardly waiting long enough to understand about the bank being robbed, and Percy's biplane being used by the thieves as a means of making a quick get-away."

Andy turned his head and looked in his cousin's face.

"Public-spirited citizen go hang!" he said, contemptuously. "After what we saw, Frank, it's easy for us to understand just what it was made Todd want the police to do all their hunting away off in the southwest."

"Yes, what do you think was his object?" asked Frank, as he held the aeroplane just about five hundred feet above the level ground, covered by forests, as in most places around to the north of Bloomsbury, though occasionally they ran across farms that looked like oases in the dessert.

"Why, that's as plain as the nose on my face," replied Andy, "and nobody ever had any trouble about seeing that, I guess. Todd wanted to get in a little bit of assistance for his friends, the hoboes who looted the bank; and he could do them the best thing ever by turning suspicion in nearly the opposite quarter. If Chief Waller could be assured that the last seen of the biplane before it vanished in the distance it was heading into the southwest, of course he'd take all his men off in that direction; and the bank robbers, hiding perhaps around the northern end of Lake Sunrise, would be free to do whatever they wanted. Do I hit about the same guess that you do, Frank?"

"You've just echoed what I had in mind," returned his cousin, "only I've had more time to think it over, and perhaps gone a little further than you could."

"As how?" demanded the other, promptly, just as Frank knew he would.

"Why, you know, it struck us as queer that these fellows should want to hang out within twenty miles of the town where they'd just made a successful raid on the bank. It would stand to reason that they'd be only too glad to cut for it, after getting possession of Percy's fine new aeroplane, and by keeping on north, reach Lake Ontario, and perhaps fly across to Canada, where they'd be safe."

"Yes, sure; we talked that over before, Frank, and came to the conclusion that either they'd met with some sort of accident to the biplane, and had to hold over till the fellow who used to be an aviator repaired the same; or else that they had some other robbery in mind, and wanted to make a double killing of it before skipping out."

"All right. You can see, then, that if Chief Waller and about all his men got on a warm clue that led them off to the southwest for a day or so, it would leave things open for the carrying out of this second scheme!"

When Andy heard his cousin say this so gravely he seemed more startled than ever.

"Say, I believe you've gone and struck the truth just as you nearly always do, old fellow, not by luck, but by figuring it out. To get the coast clear, then, this sly Todd Pemberton means to go on bringing in important news, and keeping poor old Chief Waller worked up to top-notch speed, chasing around down there after shadows! Yes, that must be the game they've got in hand; and perhaps that's what all those waves of handkerchiefs meant between the pilot of the little Mermaid, and the fellow we couldn't see, who was hidden in the bushes on Norton's Point."

"He was undoubtedly there just to give Todd the high sign when the boat passed. Both of us spoke of the fact that we'd never known the steamboat to keep so far north when making the run from Cranford, across the lake, up to the lumber camp on our northwest side. But now we can understand why; he wanted to make sure his partners in crime were ready for him to do his little share in the game; which is to send the police on a wild goose chase and leave Bloomsbury next to unprotected tonight."

"But whatever in the wide world, Frank, do you think they mean to try next?"

"I couldn't guess in a year," was the reply of the boy who manipulated the levers of the hydroplane so dextrously. "It might be any one of a dozen or two games. The bank isn't the only institution in Bloomsbury carrying a lot of money in the safe. And then there are several rich men we happen to know, who keep a little fortune about the house, in the way of money, jewelry, or curios. For all we know, these yeggs may even have an eye on your house or mine, because they could make a pretty good haul there."

"Whew!" was all Andy said just then; but his mind was undoubtedly filled with startling ideas.

CHAPTER XII

AT THE HOSKINS FARM

"Well," Andy went on to remark, presently, "I see you are turning back again in the direction of the head of the lake. I hope, Frank, you don't mean to go all the way to Bloomsbury, and put the police in possession of the few facts we've succeeded in picking up."

"That was not my calculation at all," replied the other, "in the first place, we suspect a good deal, but up to now we haven't got very much positive evidence on which to found a case. I'd like to know a little more before I get the Chief on the wire, and put him wise."

"Then when we get near the northern end of the lake perhaps you'll think it best to make a landing somewhere, and prowl around on foot, finding out what we can," Andy, continued eagerly; for he had become much worked up by this time, and was hoping that fortune would be as kind to them as on a previous occasion, which all Bloomsbury remembered very well.

"If we can only find a decent opening where we could make a get-away again, that is the only thing that bothers me," Frank replied.

"Now, I remember noticing a field near what seemed to be a lonely farmhouse; in fact there were a number of open places there, and they seemed to have Canada thistles growing in clumps, all a-bloom, as if the farmer had given up cultivating, and let things just go to rack and ruin. I was never up there myself, but from what I've heard my father say, I rather think that must be the Hoskins place. They say he consulted some fortune teller a couple of years ago, who told him he would some day discover a gold mine on his property that would make him a millionaire; and ever since the farmer has spent about all his time digging here and there, but up to now without any success at all."

"Why, yes, I remember hearing a lot about the queer old farmer myself," Frank went on to say. "He's got a wife, and a half-grown daughter named Sallie. I met her at a country dance last winter, and she's a pretty nice sort of a girl. Now, we've been on the move a good while, Andy, and perhaps we might manage to make the Hoskins farm around the dinner hour."

"A bully good idea, too, Frank, and don't you forget it!" cried the other, with considerable show of enthusiasm. "Now, I just bolted what little breakfast I got this morning, and already I feel hungry enough to eat nearly anything. And speaking generally, these country people do set a great table; though I don't know how it will be with the Hoskins, because, if they've been neglecting their farm to chase around after rainbows, they probably won't be any too flush with supplies. But any port in a storm, and I guess we'll be able to get filled up; if only we can make a landing, and find the farm."

"As I figure it out, Hoskins' place wouldn't be over a mile or so directly above Norton's Point, Andy," the pilot of the expedition continued, thoughtfully.

"Yes," Andy said, encouragingly.

"And perhaps, now, we might happen to run on some sort of a little clue there. For instance, one of those yeggmen may have wandered around, and bought some eggs or milk from the farmer's folks; because, if they've been camping out in the woods, they've had to eat all the while, you know."

"A good idea, Frank; and we'll ask, if we're lucky enough to happen around the lonely farm about meal time."

"I'm going to make it a point to be there, and as we've got some time to kill meanwhile, let's hop over to that nice landingplace at the foot of old Thunder top, and overhaul the machine again. There are a few things I'd like to tinker with, because I'm not quite pleased with the way they work; and you know, Andy, I'm a regular crank about having a motor run like a watch."

"Well, I'm getting that way mighty fast, thanks to your hints, and the knowledge of how it pays, when you're taking your life in your hands every time you go up in one of these heavier-than-air outfits," was what the other Bird boy observed, with what was a thoughtful look, for him; because, as a rule, Andy appeared to be a merry chap, and laughing much of the time.

Within half an hour they had successfully landed at the place indicated, and which had witnessed the coming and going of the young aeronauts on numerous occasions.

Here at least they could remain and take things easy while waiting for the morning to slip along, so that eleven would roll around. Little danger of their being bothered by curious persons here; indeed, the boys had never yet known a solitary man or boy to come around the place.

They could look up while lying there on their backs, and watch the fleecy clouds sailing swiftly past the lofty crown of the rocky mountain. And how vividly there came into their minds memories of lively times which they themselves had experienced up there on the summit of old Thunder top.

They spoke of them now, as they lay stretched out on the soft turf, and watched the two white headed eagles soaring far up in the blue heavens, around and around in circles, without ever seeming to flap their great wings.

Once the young aviators had engaged in a terrible conflict with those two mighty birds, on the crown of the mountain, where they had landed with their aeroplane, and been looked upon as intruders by the eagles, possibly under the belief that they entertained hostile intentions toward the fledglings in their nest that was built amidst the crags, close to the tip of the lofty peak.

Frank and Andy often spoke of that thrilling episode, but never without some sort of little shiver, because it had been a serious time with them since one blow from those powerful wings might have toppled them over the edge of the dizzy height, and sent them to their deaths.

But they had succeeded in beating their feather antagonists off by the aid of clubs which they wielded with vigor; and after the eagles learned that no harm was intended to their young by these bold navigators of the upper air currents, they came to have more respect for the strange winged thing that came humming up from the earth on more than one occasion.

When eleven o'clock came around, the boys were off again, and headed toward the northern end of the lake.

Of course they kept close down to the treetops, because, once they discovered the opening, they would wish to drop into it as easily as possible.

Suddenly Andy, who was on the lookout, while Frank paid more attention to the easy working of the motor, and the steering of the hydroplane, uttered an exclamation of satisfaction.

"I see it, dead ahead!" he remarked, in a satisfied tone. "We made a bee line to the place from the foot of the mountain, Frank. And unless I'm away off in my guess, the farmhouse lies over yonder beyond the trees; so nobody's apt to see us come down; and we can make any sort of yarn we want, to explain just why we're here right now."

"We can do that all right, without telling anything that isn't so," replied the other aviator. "The farmer doesn't know us, though Sallie will, and on that account we must be careful what we say. But the dinner's the main thing just now. And at the same time we'll try and pick up a little information, if Farmer Hoskins happens to know anything that would interest two fellows of our stamp."

He passed over the opening once, to make sure that it contained all the necessary requisites for a successful landing, and also a launching of the airship. Then, making a graceful sweep back again, Frank allowed the aeroplane to drop lightly to the ground. It landed in almost the center of the field, and both boys saw that they might get away again without a great amount of trouble.

"Fine!" was the comment of the pilot, as he jumped to the ground, and bent over to detach some part of the machinery without which the motor, as Andy always said, "would not move worth a cent." This he often took with him, just as a chauffeur might the spark plug of an automobile, rendering it helpless unless the would-be thief were prepared to supply the deficiency off-hand, which was a remote possibility that never worried Frank.

"Now for grub!" announced the hungry Andy, leading off in the direction where he had reason to believe the farmhouse lay; Frank always declared that Andy had a most wonderful nose for a meal that was preparing, and could spot a camp a mile away just by the smell of frying onions, or coffee cooking.

At any rate he proved to be a successful pilot on the present occasion, for in a short time they were passing through an abandoned grain field where the bees and butterflies were swarming about the many lavender colored flowers of the great clumps of thistles; and the smoke from the farmhouse kitchen arose just over a little knoll.

"Told you so," said Andy, as they drew near the house, and caught fragrant odors of cooking in the air.

Upon their knocking a girl came to the open door, and recognized Frank immediately as a boy she had met at the country dance the preceding winter. But nothing she said would indicate that the Hoskins, living here away from the world as they did, with the head of the house spending all his time hunting for that treasure-trove he still believed in, had heard anything to speak of about the wonderful things the Bird boys had been doing lately.

Frank was glad of this, and he just casually mentioned that they chanced to find themselves near the farm, and wondered if they could get dinner there.

So the good housewife was brought out, and with true country hospitality she immediately invited both boys to sit down with them, although saying that they were not as well supplied with the good things that used to be seen on their table before father took to boring those horrid holes all over the place, thinking to strike a coal vein, or perhaps a silver mine.

He was off now, and would not show up until night, for the farm was one of vast dimensions, and covered miles of territory.

"But we have a boarder," said Sallie, as they sat down at the table. "Sometimes he's here to meals, and again he gets so far away chasing his butterflies that he just carries what he calls a snack in his pocket. Such a queer little man he is too, with his brown glasses on, and always running this way and that with his little net in which he captures the butterflies that come to the thistles on our old barren fields. Perhaps he'll turn up while you're here. I'd like you to meet Professor Whitesides, who is from a big college, he tells us, and spending his vacation in the way he likes. Sometimes I think he's a little off up here," and she touched her head as she said this, "and that perhaps he got hurt worse than he thinks, the time he met with the accident that crippled his arm."

Somehow Andy looked up when he heard about that broken arm to find his cousin giving him the wink, while his eyebrows were elevated in a suggestive way, just as much as to say:

"Now, here's something mighty interesting already that would pay us to look into; because we know of another fellow who is troubled with a crippled arm and his name happens to be Casper Blue!"

CHAPTER XIII

THE BUTTERFLY COLLECTOR

The dinner passed off without the odd little professor showing up, although Sallie said it was nothing unusual for him, and that he was liable to appear at any time, carrying his little white hand-net, and a small handbag in which he claimed to keep the trophies of the chase that had been run down during his last campaign.

Frank wanted to get a chance to confer with his chum, and as soon as he could conveniently withdraw from the table, giving Andy a nod, he went out on the porch where he could look down the lane that led to the poor road, which in turn, after many trials and tribulations merged into the main pike.

Andy joined him there a minute later, with a question in his eye.

"Professor Whitesides!" was what Frank remarked.

"And a butterfly collector at that!" Andy went on to say, with cutting sarcasm.

"That sounds pretty rich, to me," his cousin continued. "I wonder, now, could it be possible that the other man we've heard of lately, Casper Blue, is playing a smart trick on these honest people, who would never dream that he could be anything else than he claimed."

"It would give him a splendid chance to wander around just whenever and wherever he wanted to go, and nobody to ask questions. Then, when he got hungry, why, he could drop in at the farm. Perhaps he don't like camping out as well as the other fellow; perhaps his health is too delicate to stand roughing it. Or he might have any one of a dozen other reasons for carrying on this way; always providing that this is Casper Blue."

Andy was brimful of excitement. His manner would forcibly remind one of the nervous tension that seizes upon the hounds when the scent grows strong, and they anticipate coming in sight of their quarry at any moment.

"We're taking a good deal for granted, seems to me," remarked Frank.

"Of course, but then see how queer it is that this man who calls himself a college professor, and collector of bugs and butterflies, should just happen to drop in here at the Hoskins farm, where the thistles grow so wild, and the moths and other things are to be found by thousands. We never heard of him in town, that I can remember. And then he's small in size; together with a stiff arm, that was injured in an accident; well, wasn't Casper Blue knocked out of his job as an air pilot by his arm failing him when he had to handle the levers like a flash, or have his aeroplane turn upside-down, Frank? I tell you I just feel dead sure it's our man, and that we've found the clue we want the first thing."

"Well, if we could manage to get a peep into his room perhaps we would run across something worth while?" Frank suggested.

"We might pretend to be deeply interested in butterflies ourselves," remarked Andy, "even if we don't really know one kind from another; and perhaps, if you gave Sallie a sly hint that you'd be tickled to see what sort of a collection her professor has with him, she'd let us look in his room."

"We'll make the try, anyhow," said Frank, firmly.

"But think of this Casper Blue being able to carry out the part of a learned professor, would you? That is something most yeggmen would find a pretty hard proposition, don't you say, Frank?"

"Well, stop and think a little, Andy," was the other's reply to this. "From all accounts this man isn't just a common, everyday hobo. He used to be known as something of an aviator before he met with that accident that disabled his arm, and made it impossible for him to go up again. And the fact is, I seem to remember having seen that name mentioned among a list of airmen who had been either killed, or knocked out by accidents happening to them."

"That's all right, Frank, but it takes a pretty smart man to carry out a part like he's doing."

"Didn't Larry tell us that this same Casper Blue had once been an actor before he took to the air for a living?" asked Frank.

"You're right, he did that same thing, but somehow it seemed to have slipped my mind. But you never forget a single thing, do you, Frank? And if he used to be an actor, why, of course Casper would find it easy to play this part. Perhaps he's just enjoying it the best you ever heard of. Some people are never happy unless they're hoodwinking others."

"Let's go back and find Sallie, and get to talking about butterflies and gypsy moths, and all sorts of things in that line we can think of," suggested Frank. "Then she'll believe we're head over ears interested in what her boarder is doing, and if I give her a little hint she may ask us to step in and take a peek at his room. Of course we mightn't pick up anything worth while there; and then again there's always a little chance we could."

"It's worth while, I think," declared Andy, who seldom disagreed with any proposition his cousin advanced, simply because Frank was usually so wise that he succeeded in covering the whole ground the very first thing.

So they once more left the porch, though both boys looked down the lane before going in, to make sure that the queer little butterfly collector was not coming in time to interfere with their immediate plans.

Sallie was just tidying up the diningroom when they found her. The good woman of the house seemed to have gone into the kitchen, where she was preserving some sort of fruit, or making catsup, to judge from the fragrant odors that came floating out from that part of the farmhouse.

Naturally Sallie was only too willing to enter into conversation again with two such attractive looking and bright boys as Frank and Andy Bird. She must have been aware of the fact that they were favorites among the girls of Bloomsbury; and of course also knew something about their being aviators, although both or 'them had shunned that subject carefully while at the dinner table.

And so Frank managed to gradually steer the conversation around to the subject of bug collection. He told of a friend he once had who was "daffy" along that line, and would rather capture some queer looking old night-flying hairy moth, with a death's-head sign on his front, than enjoy the finest supper, or listen to the best play.

That allowed Andy to venture the suggestion that he had taken considerable interest in butterflies himself, and always wanted to see a collection that was worth while. Of course he did not have to explain that the only interest he ever did have in the matter was when, as a very small boy, he used to chase after the fluttering insects as they went from flower to flower, until shown by his mother how cruel it was to destroy the life of such wonderfully beautiful things, that he could not restore again.

Sallie took the bait, Andy knew from the eager light that flashed upon her face. And when he saw her step over to a window, and look quickly down the lane, he turned to his cousin, and made a grimace as much as to say, "See how she fell to my little game, will you, old fellow?"

"Well," said Sallie, flitting back again, "Professor Whitesides hasn't got a very large collection; and the new specimens he gathers day after day he kept in some place, because he has no time just now to do anything with them, he says; but come up with me, and I'll show you the little case he brought with him."

"Sure we will, and I'm glad of the chance to see what valuable butterflies look like," Andy went on to remark.

"He says this little collection is a very rare one, and worth an awfully large sum of money," Sallie went on to remark, in something of a confidential tone, as if getting the boys ready to be surprised when they looked upon the possessions of the industrious professor. "And oh! if you could only hear all the queer things he's been telling us that happened to him in foreign lands, when he was spending ever so much money, and long weary months, finding these very rare specimens. Why, I just stand there, and look at them, and wonder how people can be so foolish, when it seems to me I've seen much prettier butterflies right out there in our fields where the thistles are blooming."

It seemed that the room they had given the wonderful man of science was on the ground floor, and opened off the parlor.

The two boys followed Sallie in, and noted her rather awed manner 5 evidently the professor, whether he turned out to be a fraud or the genuine article, had succeeded in arousing both her admiration and wonder.

The room was plainly yet comfortably furnished, but evidently the professor, like so many other learned savants, did not know such a thing as "order" existed, for things were simply topsy-turvy.

"He just won't let us sweep in here, or do the least thing," explained Sallie, as if she feared the boys would blame her for the looks of the room, "you know, he's so queer, and he says we might lose something that he valued very highly, thinking it was not worth keeping. But here's the little case containing those almost priceless specimens he collected abroad."

She led them to a table on which a small case rested, leaning against the wall. Frank took one look. Apparently the sight affected him strangely, for immediately he bent over closer as though to feast his eyes on those costly trophies which the college professor had collected in foreign lands.

Andy saw that his cousin was evidently having some sort of a silent laughing fit, for he shook all over though not uttering a single sound.

"What ails you, Frank?" he whispered, taking advantage of Sallie having to hurry out of the room, as her mother's voice was heard calling her in the kitchen.

"I'm tickled to death to meet an old friend again, that's all," replied Frank.

"Do you mean to tell me you've seen this wonderful collection before?" demanded the other, like a flash, as it were.

"I most certainly do; and if you stop to think, Andy, I guess you'll say the same; or perhaps, now, you didn't happen to examine the case as closely as I did, that day last spring when we crossed over to Cranford, to pick up a few rare stamps for our collection at Snyder's old curio store."

"Why, bless me, I really believe you're right; I seem to remember seeing it in the show window, now, when we were looking at the little baskets of coins," Andy hastened to remark.

"There isn't the least shadow of a doubt about it," added Frank. "Some time or other, when the notion came to this man to play the part of a butterfly collector, which perhaps the sight of the things brought to his mind, he just stepped into Snyder's store, and bought the old collection. Why, it hasn't got a single specimen that you can't find a thousand of, any day you look, through August and September."

"Right around here, you mean, Frank?"

"Right on this farm, in fact," replied the other, with a wide grin. "Think of the nerve of this learned scientist bringing this here, and telling that it represented the results of years of difficult research? You don't wonder, now, that I just had to snicker, do you, Andy?"

CHAPTER XIV

A CLUE

"That looks bad, don't it Frank?" Andy went on to remark, as he first glanced at the bogus collection of rare specimens, and then eyed his cousin humorously.

"One thing is sure, no man would go to the trouble and expense of buying even a dollar case of common butterflies unless he had some deep object in view, and you know that, Andy. This so-called professor must be a fraud, even if he doesn't turn out to be the man we think he is. Perhaps, he wanting to find out whether Hoskins had discovered that wonderful gold mine. Well, you needn't grin about it because stranger things have happened, I guess, now."

Andy ceased laughing and turned to look around the room.

"I wonder—" he began, and then stopped short.

"Now I can finish your sentence for you," said Frank. "You wonder if we could make any important discovery if we looked around here a bit, while Sallie is helping her ma do up some fruit jars or something like that?"

"Perhaps it wouldn't be just the right thing," suggested Andy, in confusion.

"Under ordinary conditions it certainly wouldn't," his cousin went on to say; "but when you've got a pretty good idea that you're dealing with a slippery hobo, actor, past-aviator, and now a bank burglar and cracksman in general, why that puts a different face on the matter, don't you see, my boy?"

"All right; let's take a look," said Andy, easily convinced that since they were really working hand in glove with the police authorities, they had a perfect right to prowl around in anybody's room, and pick up such valuable information as could be found afloat.

But after all they found nothing that looked like incriminating evidence. The fact of the matter was that the professor did not seem to own any sort of wardrobe whatever, and had nothing belonging to him save the clothes on his back, the little case of butterflies which Frank believed he had bought for a dollar over in Cranford at the curio dealer's shop, and a few bottles holding some strong smelling acids, which possibly were used to either kill the captured butterflies so they would not beat their wings out; or else to preserve certain specimens of bugs he expected to run across in his hunts.

"Nothing doing," said Andy, with considerable of disgust and disappointment in his voice.

"Come here!" remarked his cousin, softly.

"Hello! don't tell me you've found something?" and Andy crossed the floor in more or less haste.

He found Frank bending over a table at which there were writing materials—pen, envelopes, paper and a blotter.

"What's doing? Have you found the gentleman's notebook lying carelessly around, and which we can peep into, eh, Frank?"

"Not at all," came the reply. "I was only looking at this blotter."

"Whatever is there funny about that?" demanded the other, in puzzled tones, as he glanced first at the object in question, and then up at the face of his chum.

"It was a new one, or nearly so, you see! and somebody has been writing heavily, and then pressing the blotter over it," Frank went on.

"And if you could read backwards now, you might make out what they said; is that it, Frank?"

"Oh! that part is as easy as falling off a log. I held it up to the looking glass here. See if you can make it out, Andy."

Hardly had the other looked than he started to read, interjecting remarks of his own as he proceeded.

"Some words missing, looks like, Frank; let's see; 'Car on siding——'rive at 11 P.M. Wed. He says keep low, and trust to him—throw—track. Mum.' That's all I can make out, because he didn't sign any name, it seems. Whatever do you make of all that stuff, Frank?"

First of all Frank pulled out a pencil and copied the marks upon a piece of paper, which he thrust into his pocket.

"He might miss the blotter if I cribbed it, and take the alarm," he explained, as he hastened to put the article in question back on the table, lest Sallie come in at any minute and discover what they were doing, taking liberties in the room of the boarder; and then she would have to be told everything, which might work out badly, Frank feared.

"But I reckon you've got some sort of idea what that writing means, Frank?" pursued the other Bird boy, who, once he started on a subject could no more be shaken off than a bulldog.

"Of course I have, and it's given me something of a shock, too, let me tell you, Andy. First of all, you may know that this very day is Wednesday."

"The day he mentions there; to be sure it is. But Frank, can all this have some reference to another crime they mean to commit?"

"I'm afraid it does," came the reluctant reply.

"Tell me what he means by 'car, siding, track, mum,' and all that. Of course I can understand that he warns the fellow he's sending the message to to keep quiet. What car can he mean? Do you think they aim to steal some one's expensive car now—that they've gone and wrecked Percy's biplane, and must have another means for getting away?"

But Frank simply shook his head at that.

"Oh! you're away off your base there, Andy. He speaks of a car on a siding, and that can only refer to a railroad car. Now, I happen to know that they expect the pay-car to be along some time today or tonight, and it always lies there on that Jeffreys Siding, until they've passed out thousands of dollars to the men who call Bloomsbury their headquarters. Do you see now what it must mean, Andy?"

Andy gasped, and then exclaimed.

"Once more you've gone and seen through the riddle that knocked me silly, Frank. That's just what it must mean—the pay-car would offer fat pickings, all in cash; and they've held up their flight to Canada just to try and gobble it. Oh!

what a slick game, with Todd giving false information, and perhaps just leading the police further and further away from Bloomsbury tonight, so as to leave the pay-car next to unprotected. Yes, and doesn't he go on like this, 'he says keep low, and trust to him'? That must mean Todd, don't you think?"

"I read it that way," replied his cousin tersely, as he rubbed his chin in a reflective fashion; for they were now grappling with a dangerous problem, and Frank was only too well aware of the fact that a slip might upset all calculations, as well as possibly endanger their lives; since they were dealing with reckless men, and no boyish rivals like Percy Carberry and Sandy Hollingshead.

"Do you think this was meant for the other one of the bank thieves?" Andy went on to ask.

"It could hardly have been for any one else, Andy. There must have been more to the letter, but the rest dried before he blotted it."

"And that fellow is in hiding somewhere, perhaps watching the biplane, and ready to fight before letting it be retaken, because they depend on it for their get-away to the great lakes and Canada;" Andy further observed.

"Yes, just as you say," the other remarked.

"And now since we've learned this much, Frank, what are we going to do about it—try and find where the stolen biplane is, and do something so as to make it no good for their purpose; or just slip away, go round a little like we were just out for a spin, and getting back to Bloomsbury, put them wise?"

"Neither, just yet anyhow," the older Bird boy remarked. "Not the first, because it would be taking big chances, if, as we believe, one of the robbers is concealed near where the stolen biplane may happen to be lying, partly hidden with dead leaves, so it couldn't be noticed from above; and he would be apt to do something we'd find unpleasant. And as for going back and telling, we'll have to be mighty careful there."

"And why, Frank?"

"Well, to begin with, even the walls have ears, they say; and if the police were suddenly called back from their hunt to the southwest, the fact might get to the robbers; and you know what would happen then."

"Oh!" said Andy, shrugging his shoulders, "I suppose they'd just throw this second job up, and cut stick for Canada, as fast as they could make the aeroplane spin, which would be too bad for Chief Waller, and Joe Green, and the rest of that bunch at Headquarters, who are already figuring on how they'll spend their reward money they hope to get when the bank pays for rounding-up the two thieves."

"But, perhaps, if we just told our fathers, Andy, they might get a few bold men together and lay a beautiful trap for the fellows so that when they broke into the pay-car, they would be made prisoners."

"Bully idea, that, Frank, and I hope you decide to carry it out. Just to think what a pleasant surprise it would be for our butterfly collector, expecting that he was going in to gather in another lot of plunder, and then to hear a voice say to him: 'Hands up! you're our prisoners!' Oh! wouldn't I like to be Johnny-on-the-spot when that happens. Wonder if they wouldn't let us have a part in the proceedings, after we brought the news that upset the plans of the yeggmen?"

"That will do for just now, Andy, because here comes Sally again. Let's be gaping at the wonderful collection that almost cost the professor his very life in all sorts of hot countries, as well as a whole pocket full of money—if you don't care what you say."

And when the farmer's daughter did enter the room a minute later, she saw the two boys standing there, a rapt look of admiration and envy on their faces, as they stared at the little case of common local butterflies which possibly some boy had gathered together, and then disposed of for a song.

While the young aviators had in this fashion about decided on their plan of action, they saw no reason for any hurry. The day was still long, and when they felt like starting toward home it would take them but a very short time to get there.

Meanwhile, there seemed to be some sort of fascination holding them to the neighborhood of the Hoskins' farm. And when they went away a little later it would be with the idea of hanging about, and seeing if the odd little professor might not come along. Both of them thought they would like to look at him. The man who was capable of playing such a clever game as this must surely be worth seeing.

Then again, the fact that Casper Blue once upon a time had been a daring birdman had something to do with this interest on the part of Frank and his cousin, because there is always a certain fellow feeling between those who are engaged in the same dangerous pursuits. But possibly Andy on his part was hoping secretly that by spying around they might be able in some way to learn where the yeggmen had hidden the plunder they had taken from the looted Bloomsbury bank.

CHAPTER XV

WHEN CASPER CAME BACK

Although the Bird boys had more than once before proved that they possessed all the courage and daring a successful aviator must have in order to accomplish the difficult tasks hourly presented to him for solution, it must not be thought that they were reckless to any degree.

Andy might be slightly inclined that way, but Frank was an exceedingly careful navigator of the air, and by degrees his influence was even affecting his younger cousin, as example always will.

When, however, a situation suddenly arose that absolutely required a display of daring, these young air pilots were "there with the punch," as Andy termed it. They had learned how to volplane earthward from a dizzy height with absolute safety, when conditions were just right, and necessity required a quick descent. On a few occasions Frank had even been known to hazard what is known as the "death dip;" but it was only when there happened to be a good reason for taking such chances, and not merely in a spirit of dare-deviltry, such as many show aviators employ, just to send a shiver of dread through the spectators, and then laugh recklessly at the fears their boldness had aroused.

Of course they might have decided to immediately return to Bloomsbury, and give information concerning the extent of their discoveries since coming to the Hoskins' farm.

Perhaps that would have been the wisest move they could make but both boys were rather opposed to carrying it out just then.

The afternoon was wholly before them, and who could tell what change of plans the two yeggmen might make before the coming of the night? Should they get wind of the presence of the Bird boys in the vicinity possibly they would take alarm, and hurrying to their concealed biplane make for the far North with all haste; and in this way, if no one knew of their departure the intended ambuscade that night in the vicinity of the railroad pay-car would be laid in vain.

That was really what the boys feared the most—that their quarry slip off in secret, when they were far away.

Frank was indeed trying to figure out whether it would not be best after all for him to stay by the hydroplane, on guard as it were, while Andy, by using a horse, if the Hoskins happened to still possess such an animal, managed to get to another farm, where they were up-to-date enough to have a telephone in the house, by means of which he could get in touch with Dr. Bird or Judge Lawson in Bloomsbury.

Then again, there was always a slight chance that this pretended professor might have seen them descend, while he was wandering around. Once an airman, and just by instinct as it were, the eyes are almost constantly searching the heavens, perhaps for a glimpse of other adventurous craft, or it may be, signs that give warning of treacherous winds, gathering storms, or similar things that must always be of intense interest to an aviator.

And so while Casper Blue had long since given up taking hazards in a flying machine to indulge in even more dangerous business as a bank robber, still habits would cling tightly, and thus he might have seen more than the ordinary man could have done.

Of course, even though he sought the hydroplane, and found it lying there in the field, he could not very well make any use of it so long as Frank held the missing part in his possession.

But he could in a spirit of maliciousness so utterly destroy the planes, and even injure the powerful little Kinkaid engine that it would be practically fit only for the scrap-heap afterwards. And that was giving Frank more or less concern, even while he continued to linger at the farmhouse because Andy wished to prowl around a little while longer in hopes of getting some clue to the location of the cache where the thieves had hidden their plunder.

Sallie saw nothing strange in this apparent desire of Andy to hang around. She was rather a pretty little thing, and of course knew it; so that she may have believed the witchery of her attractions had more or less to do with the matter.

Even when Frank asked so many queer questions about the absent boarder, Sallie was not wise enough to understand that the boys Were much more concerned about how Professor Whitesides amused himself, where his favorite lounging places seemed to be, and all that, rather than in her pretty face and merry laugh.

Her mother must have counted on having her assistance in carrying on her task of putting up preserves in the kitchen, for once more she called to Sallie to come and lend a hand for a few moments.

This left the two boys alone again, and gave them a chance for exchanging views, which they were not slow to do.

"I guess he doesn't keep it around here, in this room, or anywhere close by," was Andy's first remark.

Frank chuckled on hearing this.

"Oh! I see that you've got your mind set on recovering what was taken from the bank. You're a mercenary fellow, Andy. But, then, since our fathers have more or less interest in the same bank, which is going to be mighty badly crippled if the cash and securities are not recovered sooner or later, why, I can't blame you much. I'd like to run across the loot myself, more than I can tell you."

"I'm only afraid that if the men are taken prisoners to night, when they come to clean out the pay-car after it arrives in Bloomsbury, they'll not have this other stuff with them, and will refuse to tell where it's hidden. That will be just as bad for the bank as if they'd got away to Canada with the swag, as the Chief calls it. I wish I knew how we could track this Casper Blue to where the other yegg is hiding near the biplane, and watch them until we saw where they had the cache. After that we could just hang around, and when they started in a power-boat perhaps for Bloomsbury, with Todd Pemberton at the wheel, we could do something to make the biplane useless to them, and then toward evening put for home ourselves."

Frank listened while the other ran all of this off, and evidently he was more or less amused at what he heard.

"It's plain to be seen that you've been doing some tall thinking and planning all this while, Andy," he remarked.

"But you'll admit, I guess, that if there was any way to carry out my scheme, it would be a jim dandy idea," the other persisted.

"Of course; but that's where the trouble lies. Even if Casper did come back, we never could track him through the woods and around the swamps without his sooner or later discovering that he was being followed, because we're not clever at that sort of thing. And once he got wind of our being after him, chances are he'd lay some trap with his mate, into which both of us would tumble headlong."

Andy scratched his head, and a look of doubt came upon his face.

"H'm! I wouldn't like that one little bit, and that's a fact, Frank," he admitted, candidly. "If we fell into their hands and were kicked around and then left tied up like a pair of mummies from the pyramids of Egypt, while they went and cleaned out that pay-car, and sailed away for Canda—oh! excuse me, if you please. Anything but that. The laugh would sure be on the Bird boys. I don't mind posing once in a while as a hero; but it would jar me a whole lot to know that people were pointing me out, and telling how nicely these wonderful Bird boys had been taken in and done for by a couple of traveling yeggs. Have it your own way, Frank, and don't pay any attention to my silly schemes.

"Your ideas are all right, Andy, but the only trouble is they are too strong for a couple of boys to carry out. I think we'd be wise to play safe. More games are won in the long run that way, than by being dashing and venturesome."

"Of course you're right, and as I've had my little fling, and got it out of my system, let's work along the sensible lines you laid out, Frank."

That was just like Andy. He might occasionally seem to yearn to break loose, and take a wild flight, but on second sober thought he nearly always came back to his cousin's way of thinking.

Sallie still remained in the kitchen, so that they were able to keep on talking without any fear of being interrupted or overheard.

"I'm wondering if Percy will ever have the chance to handle his Farman biplane again," Andy went on to remark. "He seemed to set a great store by it to offer such a nice fat reward for its return. And it's so brand new that he hasn't had much of a chance to try it out. Wasn't he mad, though, when he came racing along in that car looking for Chief Waller. He looked as red as a turkey gobbler. Just to think that while he was up there with three of his cronies trying to injure our machine, those yeggs were fixing it all up so that they could get his biplane, if they missed ours. It's a rich joke on Perc."

"Oh! I hope he gets it back again safe and sound," said Frank. "Life would be rather tame for us around home here, if we didn't have Percy to think about. For a long time, now, he's kept us guessing, and we'd feel a little lonely if he gave up flying."

"Guess you're right there, Frank, it would seem humdrum like if we didn't have to think of him every little while, and what new schemes he was planning to get the better of the Bird boys. And say, some of his games kind of dazzle a fellow, if only there wasn't so much meanness about 'em. When Perc gets to hating a fellow he doesn't stop half way, but goes the whole hog. Why, more than a few times he's given us a big scare, trying to do some stunt that would make us look small; and at the risk of sending us all down a thousand or two feet. After all, I'm beginning to believe I'd sleep sounder if Percy Carberry took to some other play, and let aeroplanes alone."

"Well, he seems just as wild about them as ever, and so I reckon he'll just keep on bothering us to the end of the chapter. But what are you looking at, Andy?" and Frank also turned his eyes down toward the fringe of quince trees that marked the old lane leading to the barnyard from the road.

"I thought I saw some one coming over there, and if it turned out to be our good friend, the profess, p'raps we'd be wise to skip out before he sighted us, Frank."

"Here, let's step back out of sight, anyhow, so as to be ready to slip away if it is our man," and Frank drew his companion around the corner of the house, from which point they could still keep watch over the lane.

Half a minute later Andy whispered:

"There, I saw him again, Frank, and as sure as anything it must be Casper. He's a little man, wearing brown glasses to keep the bright sun from his eyes, and yes, he's carrying a butterfly catcher's net over his shoulder. Shall we disappear?"

"I think that would be our best move, Andy; and lucky enough we've got the chance to slip around here, and get back of the barn before he comes along," with which the two boys hastened to follow out the plan suggested.

CHAPTER XVI

THROWING OFF THE MASK

"Do you think he saw us, Frank?" asked Andy, after they had found a place where they could peep around a corner, without being discovered.

"Well, that's more than I can say," the other replied. "We took every precaution, and unless he has mighty sharp eyes he couldn't have glimpsed us."

"And you think it's safe for us to stay here, eh, Frank?"

"Certainly," replied the other. "We're in a position to make a move any old way from here. There isn't one chance in ten of his coming around the corner; and if he does make a show of doing that, why we can be sitting here, playing mumble-de-peg, or something like that, just as if we didn't care whether school kept or not."

"Bully for that; who cares for expenses? Look, Frank, I was right, you see, for it was the little profess after all."

"Yes, sure enough. Careful now, Andy, and don't let him see you peeping. That'd give the whole thing away quicker than anything else."

They had both selected positions where they could see without attracting attention. And it was with considerable eagerness that they fastened their eyes on the figure of the small, wiry man who was sauntering along toward the farmhouse, carrying a butterfly-net across one shoulder, while with his other hand he held a queer-shaped black case, which, as Sallie said, contained his more recent captures in the way of beautiful and rare moths and insects.

"That's his stiff arm, Frank; see how he moves it—the one hanging down, I mean, with black box—good gracious! now, I wonder—"

"H'sh!" whispered Frank, "not so loud; he might hear you."

"Not with the roosters crowing like they are," said Andy confidently. "But just glimpse the black box would you, Frank?"

"I am looking," returned the other.

"He calls it the receiver for his new butterflies, but looks more like a kodak to me," Andy went on. "But d'ye know what I thought, Frank?"

"Tell me," whispered the other, still watching the professor, who had come to a stop at some little distance away, and seemed to be busily engaged looking back of him, as though laying out plans for an afternoon campaign among the bright winged butterflies.

"Why, how easy for him to tear out the inside works of a camera box like that, and make use of it for a better purpose, see?" Andy went on to say.

"Oh! now you've got a bright thought for a fact," Frank sent back, careful not to raise his voice above that cautious pitch.

"Well, it could be done; and I guess that little black box'd hold about all the money and securities that the bank lost. They say the thieves only picked out the papers they could dispose of, and left all the rest, which would indicate that the second yegg must have been in the banking line, some time or other, and knew what was what."

"H'sh! he's coming on again! Lie low, now; Andy!"

Accordingly both of them remained perfectly motionless as the professor advanced toward the house. Had he shown any disposition to head toward that particular corner Frank was ready to assume an attitude of indifference and appear to be engaged in some boyish game with his jack knife, tossing it up in the air, and causing the point of the long blade to stick upright in the ground.

But the small man with the brown glasses and the butterfly net made straight for the front porch of the house, and passed in at the door, just as though he felt perfectly at home there.

"Well, what next?" remarked Andy.

For reply the other beckoned, and started hurriedly to gain the shelter of the woodshed near by.

"What's this for?" questioned Andy, when they were once more crouched down, in a position where they could not be easily seen.

"Stop and think," answered the other; "if he just happened to look out of a window on this side of the house he'd see us easily and our suspicious actions would tell him we were on to his game. Now even if he looks he won't see anything."

"Huh! and do we stay here all afternoon just doing nothing; while p'raps he's taking a nap indoors?" grumbled the other, who wanted to be moving, and was never satisfied when not in action.

"Wait!" was all Frank would say.

Perhaps he could see further ahead than his cousin, and guessed something of what was likely to occur. They had not taken pains to warn Sallie or her mother to keep from mentioning the fact of their happening around; and chances were, that as soon as Casper Blue heard that the Bird boys had dropped in, he would become immediately suspicious.

On questioning the girl he would be apt to learn how curious Frank and Andy had seemed about him; and Sallie might even admit that they had asked to see his wonderful collection of rare and costly butterflies.

Well, if such a thing did occur, of course the keen-witted man would immediately know that the cat was out of the bag. Realizing that there must be a great hue and cry throughout the entire county just then, with reference to the yeggs who had looted the bank, he could easily imagine what had brought these boys here.

Through association with Todd Pemberton, Casper must have learned a whole lot with regard to Frank and his cousin. Being an aviator himself he would naturally take an immediate interest in boys who had given such a good account of themselves in the field of aeronautics. The attempt to steal the hydroplane in the first place before they turned to Percy Carberry's biplane proved that they knew all about the Bird boys. And so, learning of their presence would immediately give Casper warning that his hideout was no longer a secret, but that the net of the law must be closing around him.

What then?

Would he, like a desperate man, attempt to capture these venturesome lads, so as to keep them from informing the authorities at Bloomsbury? Either that, or else he would think that, since the game was up, and they could no longer loiter in the neighborhood of the aroused district in order to carry out the second part of the great scheme, they had better take to the aeroplane and vanish from view, leaving no trail behind by means of which they could be followed.

Frank had said all this in his mind when he lay there and waited to see what would turn up. He felt that they could surely afford to linger for some time, if there was any chance of learning whether the yeggmen meant to change their plans, or proceed to carry out their original scheme.

All seemed quiet at the farmhouse.

Sallie had come out on the porch, and looked rather disappointed to find that the two boys had strangely vanished. She stood there glancing around in a puzzled manner for several minutes, and then with a pretty shrug of her shoulders, and a pout of her lips whirled about and went back into the house again.

"Wow!" said Andy in a low tone, "she's got it in for you, Frank, because you dropped out of sight without even so much as saying goodbye."

But the other was thinking of weightier matters than the humor of a little coquette. He wondered whether Sallie would run across the professor and ask him if he had met two boys down the lane; which remark would excite his suspicions, and lead to other questions, now on his part.

If nothing happened inside of half an hour. Frank was of a mind to try the plan that had come to him—sending Andy off to try and reach some other farm where they would have a telephone; while he himself remained to keep watch.

That might necessitate taking Sallie into their confidence, for they would need to ask questions, and perhaps borrow a horse. On second thought Frank was now a little sorry he had not seen fit to tell the girl all. She seemed to be fairly clever, and could possibly keep a secret. At any rate, the chances of discovery would not be nearly so serious as now, when in her ignorance she was likely to blurt out all about the boys having been there, without knowing that in so doing she might be assisting clever yeggmen to avoid arrest.

The seconds moved along and changed into minutes.

If the professor had come to a window on that side of the house to look anxiously around, he must have been careful not to expose himself, for though Frank had kept a keen lookout he had failed to see anything of him.

It was getting very much of a bore to Andy. He changed his position restlessly several times, as though he wished Frank would make some sort of a move, he hardly cared what its nature so long as it meant action.

But although Andy could not see it at that moment, there were lively enough times ahead of them to please even his impetuous nature. And the passage of every minute brought the crisis closer and closer.

Once Frank believed he heard loud voices inside the farmhouse; and at the same time some one was certainly hurrying back and forth. But then possibly that might be only Sallie, obeying another call from the kitchen, where the good woman was so busily engaged with her canning operations.

Something like twenty minutes must have passed since the boys made their change of base. To Andy it was much longer, for he felt the time pass as though it had leaden wings.

Then Frank, watching, saw some one come hastily out of the front door, pass quickly down to the path, and move away in the direction of the lane.

"He's going off, Frank!" exclaimed Andy, all excitement, just as though he half expected that his companion would give the word that meant an immediate pursuit.

"Yes; keep quiet, Andy!"

"But he'll give us the slip, don't you see?" persisted the other.

"Let him, then; we can't help it. You can see that he's made quite a change in his looks, as though he's thrown the mask off, and doesn't expect to play the part of a collegeman and a bug collector any more," Frank whispered.

"That's so, he hasn't got the brown glasses on, and that old butterfly net is missing; but Frank, just notice, won't you, how he hangs to that little camera-like black box. Say, perhaps I was right after all; perhaps Casper Blue is carrying all that stuff cribbed from the Bloomsbury bank, inside the same."

The two boys crouched there behind the woodshed and by cautiously peeping around the corner could watch the late boarder of the Hoskins hurrying down the lane, as though he had received a hasty summons from the president of his college demanding an immediate return.

He seemed uneasy and suspicious, for several times he turned his head and looked this way and that, as though half expecting to discover some person ready to dispute his departure. And Frank also noted the way one of his hands had of keeping in the pocket of his short coat; just for all the world as though he might be grasping some sort of pistol that was concealed there.

CHAPTER XVII

SALLIE RIDES BAREBACK

"And now what's our next move?" demanded Andy, who generally found it very nice to let Frank do all the planning, though capable of taking hold himself when forced to do it.

Fortunately Frank had a great way of figuring out what he would do under certain conditions. This gave some sort of assurance when difficulties arose; for there was little time lost in fixing things up so as to have a programme.

"No use trying to follow after him, to begin with," he declared.

"Why do you say that?" his cousin wanted to know.

"First of all, it would be a bad business, because he's on his guard, and a desperate man," Frank went on to explain. "You can see that he's ready to pull out a weapon of some sort at the first warning. And we settled that we didn't want to fall into the hands of these two bad men. So we'll have to arrange things along a different line. And anyhow there's no terrible hurry, because I rather guess they've got the biplane hidden some distance away from here. It would take half an hour, perhaps much more, before they could get out. And we can reach our craft in a few minutes, if pushed."

"Yes, that's all so, Frank; but go on, and tell me the rest."

"I was thinking that we ought to try and let our folks know how things are going with us, so that if we have to cut out after these yegg aviators they'll know where we've gone. Suppose, now, you hunt Sallie up, and try to explain it all to her just as fast as you can."

"Who, me? Oh! well, I guess I can do it, if I have to. But what will you be doing all that time, Frank?"

"I want to write a message to either your father, or else Judge Lawson, whichever she can get on the phone," replied the other, immediately hunting in his pockets for pencil and paper, which he made it a habit to carry around with him always.

"She—say, do you mean Sallie, Frank?"

"No other. You must coax her to saddle up a horse, and make for the nearest neighbor where they've got a phone; get that, Andy?"

"But do you think she will?" asked the other, dubiously.

"I'm dead sure of it," came the confident reply. "Sallie has a touch of romance in her make-up; and besides, she'll be so mad to think of that man deceiving her mother that she'll want to have him caught. Get along with you, now, Andy, and fix it all up inside of ten minutes. I'll have the message written out by that time, so she can start, if there's such a thing as any kind of a horse around this wreck of a farm."

And so Andy, glad at least to have something to do, hurried toward the house to look for the country girl.

Left alone, Frank continued to write as plainly as he could what he wanted those in Bloomsbury to know about matters in general. He used as few words to cover the case as possible, but gave the leading points, even to stating his fear that the scoundrels who had robbed the bank, and were plotting to also make a descent on the pay-car of the railroad that night, had now taken the alarm, and would be off in the stolen biplane.

In that event Frank wanted the police in Bloomsbury to know that he and Andy had started in pursuit; though what they could do to apprehend the rogues of course he was in no position to declare.

By the time he had this finished to his satisfaction he heard voices near by, and was glad to see his cousin coming, accompanied by Sallie.

The girl looked duly excited, just as Frank had expected. There were a thousand questions in her eyes, but he cut all this short.

"We can't stop to tell you any more now, Sallie, but we promise to drop in again after it's over, and explain all that seems queer to you now. Here's the message that we want to get to Bloomsbury the worst kind, and as quick as you could get on a horse and ride to the nearest neighbor who has a phone in the house. You'll do this for us, won't you, Sallie?"

Few people could say no to Frank once he wore that winning smile, and Sallie immediately declared that she was ready to do anything he suggested.

"To think of that little scoundrel fooling us all, and pretending to be a college professor!" she remarked, indignation flashing from her black eyes.

"I hope you've got a horse," said Frank, sticking to the business in hand.

"Oh! yes; we have one left that might do," Sallie answered.

"Then let's get him saddled right away," Frank went on.

"Can't," she snapped back, "ain't such a thing as a saddle around here any more. But I'm a country girl, you know, and I can ride bareback all right. A halter's the only bridle I want, Frank. Give me the message, and I'll see that it gets to somebody in Bloomsbury."

"And here's some money, Sallie," the other went on.

"What! do you think—"

"There might be something to pay, you know, and we can't afford to take chances when there's so much at stake. Thank you a thousand times for helping us out, Sallie. Now, please get the horse. I'd like to see you started before we pull out, because we may have to chase after these fellows in our aeroplane, if they take a notion to fly away."

The girl hastened to lead the way into the stable where they did find an apology for a horse, which she immediately unhitched, and led outside.

"Hope she doesn't happen to run across that man on the way, because he might wonder what was taking her off like that, and do something to turn her back. What if he found your message on her, Frank?" and Andy, as he said this, turned an anxious gaze upon his cousin.

But Frank shook his head.

"I saw him dodge out of the lane and take to the woods," he remarked, "as though he knew of a short-cut across lots to the place where his friend and the biplane were hidden. No danger of his seeing Sallie, so don't mention it to her. Wait, I'll give you my hand to help you up, Sallie!"

But the country girl had led the horse alongside the drinking trough, and was on his back in a jiffy, long before Frank could come across.

"Goodbye, and good luck, boys!" she called back, as she gave the horse a switch with the end of the halter, and was off at a lumbering pace.

They stood there a minute or so watching the girl flying down the lane. She turned around once, and waved her hand at them, while her long hair blew behind in a cloud. Frank would not soon forget the sight of Sallie Hoskins going to carry the news to a point where it could be telephoned in to town—news that would cause a tremendous wave of excitement to pass over the whole of Bloomsbury.

"Hurrah! that's done, and well done too, Frank, I say!" exclaimed Andy, turning on his cousin with a face that plainly said, "What's next on our programme?"

"Before we pull out I guess we owe it to the good woman to tell her something of the truth, for I don't believe she knows a single thing about it from Sallie or the professor. So come along to the kitchen with me, Andy. Then we'll chase off to where we left our aeroplane, and stand ready for anything that may happen."

The two of them quickly reached the kitchen door. Inside they found Mrs. Hoskins, tired looking and red of face, still busily engaged with her canning operations; for peaches were ripe, and tomatoes needing immediate attention if she hoped to lay away her customary stock for the coming winter.

She came to the door where it was cooler, a look of rising curiosity on her patient face. And Frank started in to tell what he thought necessary. She was at first much worried to learn that she had been innocently harboring a criminal under her humble roof; but Frank soon allayed her fears on that account.

He also told her how Sallie had consented to ride over to a neighbor to send a telephone message for him, so that the good woman might not be worried over her absence.

And now, having done what he considered his duty, Frank began to think it might be the part of wisdom for himself and his cousin to consider their own affairs, and make for the spot where their hydro-aeroplane lay in the field.

"Oh! I do hope they are caught," said the farmer's wife. "Just to think of that easy talking little man being a desperate criminal! I shall be afraid to stay all alone in the house after this."

"Listen, Frank; somebody's shouting out there. What if both of those yeggs are coming back to get us?"

Andy had clutched the sleeve of his cousin's coat when saying this; but Frank did not need to be told that something like excitement was bearing down upon them.

"Oh! it's Jerry, my husband!" exclaimed Mrs. Hoskins just then, "and he seems to be dreadfully excited, too. Listen to him calling to me! I wonder what could have happened. What if he's gone and cut himself badly, always digging and making holes in the ground, since that silly old fortune teller said he would find a mine on the farm. And here he comes too!"

Just then a figure came staggering around the corner of the house. It was the old farmer, plainly tremendously excited, and although weak and almost out of breath from running, trying to tell her something.

"It's there, Jennie—found it, wife—ain't had all my work for nothin' I tell you! A vein of hard coal, think, enough to make us all rich! D'ye hear that, Jennie, girl, rich! Gimme a drink of water, for I'm nigh dead from runnin' to tell you the great news. Who's these boys, wife? Where's Sallie at?"

Frank would have liked very much to remain and hear the particulars of the farmer's good luck in locating a vein of coal on his property; but time would not permit. He only hoped Hoskins was not mistaken, for traces of coal had been known to exist around that neighborhood for some time, though up to now none had been found in paying quantities for mining purposes.

"Come on, Andy, we'll have to be skipping out. Please tell your husband all you know about what's happened, Mrs. Hoskins. Hope you have struck it rich, sir."

With that Frank hurried off, Andy trailing behind. The farmer stared after them as though hardly knowing what to make of it all; but they could hear the good woman begin to explain, and had no doubt she would be able to satisfy his reasonable curiosity.

For the time being the Bird boys must forget all about what lay in the past, because it was the future that should interest them wholly. They had reached a point in the hunt where perhaps a sudden change of plans would be necessary; particularly if those they followed had taken the alarm, and were ready to shake the dust of this section of the country from their shoes.

Away from the farmhouse hurried the two young aviators, making as near a bee line for the field where they had left their aeroplane as they could possibly manage, and all the while searching the sky for signs of the other flying machine.

CHAPTER XVIII

AN AEROPLANE CHASE

"Here it is, and everything seems all right!" remarked Andy as they reached the field, and found the hydro-aeroplane just where they had left it.

"Yes, no one has disturbed a thing, which I think is lucky for us," Frank went on to say, as he proceeded to put back the small part he had taken away with him, and thus place the machine in perfect condition for business.

Andy moved about, looking to see that all obstacles threatening to interfere with a successful launching were removed from in front of the waiting aeroplane.

So minutes passed, until at least ten had crept by since their coming. Frank had everything tuned up, and knew of not the least chance where he could improve the conditions of planes or motor, for all seemed to be as nearly perfect as they could be made.

Both boys cast frequent glances aloft, and as a rule toward that particular quarter where they presently expected to see something moving. They were keyed up to a pretty lively pitch of excitement, though Frank did not show it half as much as his younger cousin, who was always affected this way.

Then suddenly Andy called out:

"There she rises, Frank! Oh! look at them boring up, will you, in that corkscrew spiral way! Tell me that Casper Blue doesn't know his business; Perc will never get as much out of his biplane as that old and experienced aviator means to. Are we going to follow suit, Frank?"

"Get aboard!" came the prompt answer; and it was almost laughable to see how nimbly Andy obeyed this order.

Frank lost no time in starting, and they went away with a rush, passing over the abandoned field that was now given up pretty much to thistles and burdocks, with a sprinkling of iron-weeds.

It was rather rough sledding, to be sure, and as the bicycle wheels pounded over the turf the boys had to hold on to keep their seats.

But when sufficient momentum had been acquired, Frank elevated the fore plane, and immediately there was the greatest relief felt; for they began to rise in the air, and all that terrible bumping stopped for good. The change was wonderful, and it felt as though they were gliding on velvet.

"We're off!" exclaimed Andy, exultantly.

Frank said nothing. He did not possess quite the same sanguine nature that his cousin had. Andy seldom allowed thoughts of possible disaster to annoy him, but on the other hand Frank was always trying to head off trouble.

He realized that with this launching of their new hydro-aeroplane they would be entering upon an extra hazardous game, the outcome of which no one could foresee. The two men whom they expected to follow must be desperate fellows, who would resort to almost any hazard rather than allow themselves to be caught.

And it was not an amateur aviator like Percy Carberry who was opposed to them now, but one who had had long experience in the art of harnessing a flying machine to do his bidding.

Once they left the ground behind them, Frank started to spiral upward much in the same way the others had done. One thing he was glad of, and this was the presence of Andy alongside. Casper Blue might be a daring air pilot, but with his companion a perfect greenhorn in all that pertained to the art, he would be more or less handicapped. A sudden incautious movement on the part of the novice might prove the undoing of the precious pair.

Once they had risen to a certain height, and the aeroplane was turned so as to follow the other air craft, which was speeding away, headed directly into the north. Of course, those aboard must know that they were being chased. They could not have failed to see the hydroplane, (as it is generally called, though the true word to cover it would be hydro-aeroplane) even before it left the field, once they started to ascend.

"Well, we're off at last!" commented Andy, in a satisfied tone, when the course had been taken, and they were following directly after the fugitive air craft.

"And let's hope we'll come out of this adventure as luckily as we have on other occasions," remarked sober Frank.

"Wonder if Perc happens to be looking this way right now," Andy went on to say. "Chances are, that he's got his old field glass leveled, and is searching the heavens right along, in hopes of locating his lost machine. And say, if he does glimpse this fine parade right now, can't you see him turning green with envy to think of another glorious chance coming to the hated Bird boys. Oh! my, oh! me! but it would be gall and wormwood to Perc. Just as like as not he'd take a fit!"

But Frank was not giving any time to such thoughts as these. More serious affairs engaged his attention. When once he left the firm footing of the solid earth, and invaded the upper currents where up to lately man had never traveled, save in a drifting balloon, he always put levity aside, and paid strict attention to business.

The panorama below them was constantly changing, and the boys could not but admire the pictures thus presented to their gaze. No matter how often one may go up a thousand feet or more above the earth, it is next to impossible to weary of the wonderful scenes that keep passing constantly in review as the buzzing motor keeps carrying the aeroplane along over plain, valley, hills, forests, rivers, and villages or towns that chance to lie in the route.

To Andy it was all somewhat in the nature of a grand picnic, for his nature was not one to contemplate peril at a distance. Had he and Frank just come out for an hour's spin he could not have shown more delight, as they went whirling through space, with that rival flier a mile or two ahead.

"Do you think we're gaining on them?" asked Andy, after some time had elapsed, and the country below began to get unfamiliar, proving that they had now come beyond the range of any previous trip taken to the northward of Bloomsbury.

"I don't know for sure," replied his cousin. "Sometimes I think we are, and then again I'm a little in doubt. Suppose you get the glass out, and see what they're doing, Andy?"

"Well, I'm a great one, forgetting all about that bully marine glass." As he said this Andy hastened to feel for the article in question, which was always kept handy, because there never could be any telling when they might want to use it in a hurry.

"Go slow; no use rocking the boat," sang out the pilot, who was forever cautioning his companion with regard to quick motions when seated in such a delicately balanced contraption as a biplane. "It's a good thing that we've got that new fool-proof contrivance that Mr. Wright invented, on this machine right now, because only for that you'd be giving me more than a few scares when you swing from one side to the other so quickly."

A minute later, and Andy, who had been looking through the glasses, spoke again.

"It's a little hard to cover them steadily, because they keep rising and dipping just like we are; but I can see that little Casper Blue, and the man alongside of him is a much larger chap."

"Of course it's Casper who's piloting the biplane?" remarked Frank.

"Yes, and he knows the ropes, let me tell you. I don't believe there are many professional birdmen today who can go ahead of that man. I only wish you could take a squint through here, and watch how he manipulates the levers, in spite of that stiff arm of his. Only for that, and he'd still be in the harness, and doing stunts that'd have Beachy left far behind."

"Either that, or else he'd be buried," remarked Frank, drily.

"Oh! well, the less we have to say about that the better I'll feel, Frank. If you're going in for aviation at all you've just got to forget all about being in constant danger; though I hope I'll never get so I'll be reckless like Perc Carberry. But Frank, sure we seem to be picking up a little on that crowd. And from the way they keep looking back all the while, I guess they know it too."

"Perhaps we are," Frank went on to say, "but if I really thought so I'd cut down a peg or two in our speed."

At that Andy set up a howl; at least he voiced his objection.

"Well, that's a queer stunt for you to do, I must say, Frank. Here we are chasing after our game, and the very first time we believe we're gaining some, you inform me you mean to cut down our speed. Is that the way to win the game, tell me?"

"But we don't want to come up with them while we're booming along like this, you understand," ventured Frank, as he gently moved a lever just a trifle; "this sort of racing is a lot different from what you'd do on the ground down there. Suppose we did come abreast of that biplane right now, what good would that do us? Could we put out a hand and arrest the yeggmen? Wouldn't it be more likely that such desperate men as these must be, would try some sort of game looking to disable our craft, and sending us tumbling down to our death? No, excuse me from coming to close quarters up here with such hard cases. Honest now, Andy, if they began to circle around as if they meant to turn on us, I'd think it my duty to run!"

"Oh!" exclaimed Andy, "you mean you'd coax 'em to follow us back to Bloomsbury, and then give themselves up, is that it, Frank? Oh! but you're a cunning chap, sure you are. But on the level now, what is our game, if it doesn't mean we're going to overtake 'em?"

"I'll tell you, Andy. We ought to keep following after them as far as we can, and in that way learn where they drop. If we get a chance to send down an occasional message to be sent on to Bloomsbury so much the better. I've written several such out, and have the cord to tie them to weights. Given a chance, when we're passing over some town perhaps we can get one such message sent on home. Even that would tell them where we were, and what the chances are."

"Great game, Frank! Suppose you let me have those messages, and I'll be amusing myself getting the same ready to heave, when you say the word. We c'n play that this is a war game, and we've been sent out to drop bombs on the fortifications of the enemy. We've done it with rocks, and we can throw pretty straight; so it seems to me we ought to get some sort of fun out of it all around."

Frank told him where he could find the written messages in his outer pocket; and for some time Andy was quiet, busying himself in fastening some sort of anchor to each piece of paper, sufficient to carry it earthward, despite the breeze that at the time might be blowing.

All at once Andy noticed that they were going quite slowly in comparison with the pace they had lately been "hitting up."

"What's happening, Frank?" he exclaimed, almost alarmed lest some accident had befallen the reliable little motor, which up to now had never failed them, no matter how great the call upon its resources. "Why are we slowing up? Is there something gone wrong, and must we own up to being beaten?"

"Look ahead at the biplane!" was all that Frank replied.

CHAPTER XIX

DROPPING A "BOMB!"

"Oh! we've started to swoop down on them! Honest to goodness, I don't believe they're more 'n half as far ahead as they were, Frank!" cried Andy, thrilled by the sight of the other biplane being so near.

"Just about that," said Frank, quietly, the busy motor having decreased its merry hum, so that they could talk without raising their voices very much.

"Then you must have let out an extra kink, did you, Frank, when I was busy with my bombs?" demanded the other.

"Oh! no," came the answer, "the fact of the matter is, Andy, they have dropped off a lot of their speed, and that's how we covered space quicker."

"Something gone wrong with Percy's new Gnome engine, then, has it; and he blew his horn so about what wonders it was going to do? Huh!" and Andy chuckled in his boyish delight.

"No, I don't believe that is the reason they've slackened their speed, Andy."

"Trying to save gasolene, then?" pursued the other.

"Hardly that, either, Andy."

"Oh! now I see what you mean, Frank; the poor old greenhorn's got cold feet, and is making Casper slow down. He thinks that there's less chance of a tumble if the speed is reduced; just as if that could make any particular difference."

"I reckon you're away off yet," persisted Frank.

"Then, for goodness' sake won't you tell me what they have cut notches out of their speed for; because I'm all balled up, and blessed if I can think of another thing! Oh! look at that, Frank! Sure as anything I saw a puff of smoke then. There must be something the matter with their engine, and they're getting scared. I wouldn't be surprised a mite to see them settle right away, and try to land."

"Well, you saw smoke all right, and if you'd listened sharp, you'd have heard a sassy little bark at the same time, Andy."

"A what, Frank?"

"Call it a snarl, then. Take up your glasses, Andy, and look; while I drop out even a little more of our speed, so we'll fall back further."

Hardly had Andy clapped the glasses to his eyes than he gave vent to an exclamation of mingled amazement and alarm.

"That greenhorn is looking this way, Frank, and as sure as goodness he's pointing at us right now. Oh! he did something then, for I saw another puff of smoke, and it came right from his hand. Why, he's shooting at us, Frank! That must be a gun he's got in his hand, and he's trying to hit us! If our motor didn't keep up such a constant whirl we might have heard the whine of that lead when it went singing past us!"

"Yes, perhaps we might," Frank went on to say, composedly.

"But what can we do?" demanded the other, nervously.

"Nothing more than decrease our own speed as often as they do, and play the game of tag backwards. If they get going it too strong, why, just as I said before, I'll turn tail, and head back toward Bloomsbury, daring them to follow, which you can be sure they won't, because our town is a mighty unhealthy place just now for Casper Blue and his pal. There! he fired again."

"That makes three times he's tried it, Frank!"

"And I guess he can try the other three without doing us any damage, Andy."

"You believe that, do you?" asked the one spoken to.

"Sure thing," Frank replied positively. "Why, it would be one chance in ten thousand that he could strike any part of our aeroplane at that distance, going as both of us are, and with only a revolver. I'd be willing to let him blaze away all day, without being a bit afraid. But I'm bound that the two air crafts must keep at least this distance apart."

The man in the other airship did fire three more times, but without any success whatever. And as though the rival navigator realized that Frank's tactics would effectually prevent his coming into closer contact with the pursuing craft, he no longer tried to close in, but increasing his speed, was quickly about the old distance away.

Whereupon Frank Bird also hit up the pace cautiously.

"That's the ticket!" cried out Andy, presently. "I guess we're holding our own again now. For a little while I began to be afraid that they were going to just make us take their dust, and give us the merry ha-ha, vanishing in the distance. But now I know you've got the twist of the thing down fine, Frank, and can haul up on the biplane, or drop back, just as you feel like."

For a long time they kept on, neither saying anything, for talking is always more or less of an effort when speeding along in an aeroplane, with the wind striking one in the face.

Frank had had no time to fully adjust the muffler which he usually wore about his neck when about to soar to a dizzy height, so he would have to do the best he could; and besides, there was little chance of the other aeroplane venturing to bore upward to any unusual degree, all the efforts of the bank thieves being directed toward making their escape.

He did have his goggles adjusted, however, which was a good thing, since his eyes must have watered very much from the cold air; and this is considered an ever present source of danger to one who manipulates the levers of a mile-a-minute aeroplane.

"We seem to have dropped a good deal lower, Frank," remarked Andy, after another space of time had elapsed.

"Yes," remarked the pilot, tersely.

"And I'm looking now for a good chance to make use of one of my bombs; don't you think it's about time to try the scheme out?" Andy continued.

"Just as you feel like," replied Frank.

"Then at the very next town, or place that looks like it had telephone connection with the outside world, I'm going to have a try. Might have done it when we passed over that last place where the people were all waving things up at us, and we could just hear a confused shouting. I bet you, Frank, they just thought this was a regular air contest, with a prize offered to the winner."

"Well, it is," observed the other. "If we win, we take back our prisoners; and on the other hand, if they come out first best they get away to Canada with their liberty and their plunder. Yes, it's a race, all right, Andy, a test of skill and endurance; and perhaps the best man will win."

"Then I know who that will be," declared Andy, enthusiastically.

"Don't be too sure," warned Frank, though it must have pleased him to know that he possessed the fullest confidence of his cousin and chum, who had been his constant companion on so many expeditions, and must understand him like a book.

"What if they keep everlastingly at it, and night comes on?" asked Andy, presently.

"Well, there's the moon, though I don't like chasing along this way after sundown; and if we're put to it, we've got our fine search-light, you must remember," Frank replied.

"There, I believe we're going to pass right over another town, Frank!"

"It does look that way, for a fact," admitted the other. "Casper doesn't see any reason why he should bother changing his set course due north because he happens to pass a few towns away up here in the northern end of the State. Let the people stare all they want to. He's been used to having crowds gape at him, you know, and rather likes it. Besides, if he gets away, what does it matter?"

Andy prepared himself for the little job he had on hand.

As he had practiced throwing stones from the aeroplane while at a great height, just to see how near he could come to hitting a certain place far below, so as to ascertain what chance aviators would have of making bombs tell in war times, the boy believed he would be able to drop his message pretty accurately in some open place, close to where the townspeople were clustered. And seeing it fall, some one would be sure to hurry over to secure the mysterious object.

"Here goes our old broken wrench, which has been hanging around so long!" declared Andy, as, leaning carefully over, he measured distances with his eye, and suddenly let the object slip, taking care to make all allowances for their speed.

This is more of a trick than most boys would suppose. The next time you are on a speeding electric car throw a stone at a telegraph pole just as you are passing it, and see how much beyond the missile will alight, because of the momentum it received because of the fact of its starting from the moving car.

Andy had this pretty well figured out, and knew just when to launch his weighted message. He turned his head, and tried to follow it downward as well as he was able because of the fluttering white paper.

"It's going straight there, Frank, I do believe!" he exclaimed, as he managed to get the powerful glasses up to his eyes, and fairly followed the progress of the message, though quickly losing it again. "Yes, and the crowd there on the green must see it coming, because already a bunch of boys has started to jump that way. They'll find it easy enough, Frank. Now, what d'ye think of that for a successful bomb throw?"

"Good enough for you, Andy," was the hearty response. "And we'll have to take it as a sign that we're going to come out of this scrape as we generally do, with our colors flying."

Frank usually allowed himself to feel the fullest belief in his own abilities; at the same time he always wished to avoid over-confidence.

Again time passed on, and the hum of the busy motor was the only sound that came to the ears of the two young aviators. They were again making nearly full speed; though Andy felt pretty confident that, had it been necessary for Frank to coax an additional unit or two of "hurry" from the gallant little Kinkaid engine, it would respond to his efforts.

"My! but we must have covered a lot of distance since we started," was the next remark from Andy. "How long do you suppose we've been going, Frank?"

"Look and see. It was just five minutes after one when we left the field on the Hoskins farm, Andy."

"Two hours, Frank; now, what d'ye think of that? Why, I never would have believed it if you'd told me. Do you think my watch has jumped on ahead?

"No, because we've been hustling right along all of that time, I guess, Andy."

"Keeping everlastingly at it, and headed due north all the while," said Andy.

"As straight as a die; they never varied their course even a little bit, as far as I could see," the pilot declared.

"But we've covered an awful lot of apace, Frank!"

"I guess you're right there," admitted the one addressed.

"And, Frank, if we keep on this way, and nothing happens, we ought to sight the big lake away; ahead there inside of 'half an hour more, I should think?" Andy ventured to say, and he was thrilled when his companion, turning toward him just at that moment, went on to say:

"Perhaps in less time than that, Andy; with the glasses you might glimpse it even now!"

CHAPTER XX

OVER LAND AND SEA

"Are you joshing me, Frank?" demanded the other Bird boy, as he swung eagerly around, so as to fix his glasses upon the far off horizon ahead of them.

"I certainly am not, Andy; but please be more careful how you move. You gave me a punch in the ribs just then that sent a cold shiver all over me. Don't forget that we're not stretched out on the ground under an apple tree taking an afternoon doze. Well, what do you see?"

"Frank, I do believe you're right about that lake business!" exclaimed Andy.

"Then you can see it?" asked the other, himself more than anxious, because of the fact that the fleeing bank robbers who had stolen the biplane of Percy Carberry apparently intended to escape over the line into Canada, even if to accomplish their purpose they had to daringly cross Lake Ontario, many miles wide, a feat as yet only successfully done by one or two bold fliers of national repute.

"I sure can; and the way we're heading it's a dead open-and-shut thing that we're just going to swing out over the water before another hour passes. Whew!"

Andy finished his sentence with this significant exclamation. It was as though not only the novelty of the thing but its thrilling nature staggered him. The Bird boys had flown under many strange conditions, but as yet they had not made a water flight.

There is and always must be a vast difference between passing over the land, with its forests, hills, valleys, plains, cities and villages, to starting out over a wide stretch of inland sea, with only the tumbling waves far below, and new as well as untried currents of air to meet and conquer.

More than a few times Andy Bird had expressed a wish to have just such an experience. It would be a novelty, something entirely new in their line, and which would give them possibly delightful thrills.

But now that the chance seemed opening up before them, he found himself viewing it with considerable apprehension, as well as delight.

Of course it made considerable difference that they should be chasing after a desperate pair of rascals, rather than simply trying to accomplish a flight from United States territory to that belonging to Canada. There was always the chance that these men might turn upon them, and succeed in doing something to injure the hydroplane, causing it to drop into the midst of that inland sea.

Strange how small things often insist upon thrusting themselves forward when some sort of peril threatens. The very first thing Andy seemed to think about was the fact that they did not happen to have any life preservers aboard the craft. Not that there was one chance in a thousand they would ever need such things around Bloomsbury, though there was Lake Sunrise to be reckoned with; but just then it struck the boy that every well equipped aeroplane ought always to carry a couple of rubber rings along, which, in moments of dire necessity could be blown full of air, and would serve to sustain wrecked aviators until help came.

He even decided to mention this fact to his cousin, after this voyage was concluded. It loomed up as large as the Rock of Gibralter just then, even as a dream may at the moment of awaking, but which later on begins to lose its realistic effect until it seems next door to silly.

"They don't show the least sign of changing their course, do they, Frank?" Andy remarked after another spell of time had passed.

"Not that you could notice," replied the other, composedly.

Andy derived more or less comfort from this way his chum had of keeping his head even under the most trying conditions. When his own nerves were fairly quivering with excitement, it always steadied Andy to turn and see that Frank was as cool and calm as though nothing were amiss. More than a few times in the past it had caused the more hot-headed Bird boy to conquer his own weakness, and do himself credit in some difficult feat that became necessary. Example is a splendid thing to lead any boy along safe roads. Words may be forgotten in the trying moment; but when he actually sees the thing done before his very eyes, it is indelibly impressed upon his mind.

"About how long will it be before we get there?" Andy asked again; for he was forever wanting to know, when he had any misgivings about his own capacity for reaching a reasonable conclusion.

"Do you mean before we leave the land, and commence our voyage across the lake?" Frank inquired.

"Yes, that's it—more than half an hour, at the speed we're going now?" continued the other.

"Just about, I should say," Frank replied, after carefully measuring distances with his eye. "We are up pretty high, and can cover a tremendous range, you know, so we first glimpsed the lake when we were a long ways off. It may be all of forty miles away right now; and as we must be clipping along at the rate of eighty, with the breeze favorable behind us, why, half an hour ought to see us there."

Andy fell silent again.

Many times did his eyes travel from the distant water to the earth below them; and then follow this up with an uneasy stare at the other aeroplane that was flying along far ahead of them. The whole solution of the problem of course lay in the hands of the man who controlled the destinies of that stolen biplane. Would he really have the nerve to attempt a flight across that great body of fresh water, aiming to land on foreign shores, from which he could not easily be extradited?

Frank seemed to think that such was undoubtedly the intention of Casper Blue, the little man who had been actor, aviator, and yeggman in turn, during the course of his adventurous life.

He had already proven beyond any doubt that he was a capable airman, even though he did have a crippled arm. Never had the Bird boys seen an aeroplane handled with more extraordinary skill and dash than was the one that had been stolen from the hangar of Percy Carberry.

No, unless something unexpected happened to disturb the plans of the fugitive yeggmen inside the next half hour, they plainly meant to launch out on a voyage across the lake, possibly thousands of feet above its surface, and perhaps among the very clouds.

Not once did Andy dream of asking his cousin whether in this event he considered it the part of wisdom for them to follow the men who were doubly risking their lives in this mad effort to escape with their booty.

He knew Frank only too well to doubt his willingness to undertake such a trip as this. In times gone by, and especially when they were down in South America with their aeroplane, seeking Professor Bird, who had been lost, with the balloon in which he was conducting experiments on the isthmus, they had bravely faced just as serious perils as this promised to be; yes, and wrenched victory from the jaws of apparent defeat more than once.

Hence, it was a foregone conclusion that if Casper Blue attempted the difficult feat of flying across the lake, after being in the air several long hours, the two Bird boys were determined to keep following after him. It seemed like a game of "conquer," which Andy remembered so well; where the rival aviator dared to go they must follow, or acknowledge his superiority as a bold airman, something neither of them felt like doing.

Frank had figured it all out while he was speeding along so smoothly.

So far as he could see everything was working as easily as could be; the motor never missed, and was running like a charm, just as though it could keep this up everlastingly in an endurance test. And besides, the wind, what there was of it at present, seemed to favor them most positively, because it was at their backs.

So far as appearances went the conditions were ideal for the crossing of the great lake that was now showing up ahead most grandly.

Andy drew in big breaths, and tried to keep from quivering with delight, mingled with just a little nervousness. Here was a new experience about to come to them; and one that they were not apt to soon forget. As a boy Andy delighted in novel sensations; and as an ambitious aviator he yearned to experience all the glorious possibilities that open up to the one who has the pluck and the nerve to attempt them.

They could see a town in plain sight, though they had gradually ascended since Andy cast his bomb so successfully. Perhaps his little game of opening communications with the earth below had been observed by one of those in the leading airship; and in order to prevent another attempt, this gradual ascent had been immediately carried out.

But Frank fully expected to see the rival aeroplane begin to drop as they drew near the border of the fresh water sea. Since just then there was no squally wind near the surface of the water, which they wished to avoid by remaining thousands of feet high, the chances were that Casper Blue would soon commence to use his deflecting rudder, and begin to descend in wide spirals; or else, with the daring of an old and skilled air navigator, shut off power, and volplane down in a slant that would thrill any spectator as nothing else could, until the required distance had been covered, when he would again bring the shooting aeroplane on a level basis, and resume his forward progress.

Whatever he did Frank was ready to imitate.

He had the fullest confidence in his own ability to accomplish the most difficult feat that would be required.

"Steady yourself, now, Andy," he cautioned; "because they're going to change the going pretty soon, I take it. Better put that glass away, and be ready to give me a lift if I need it. Watch and see if they don't drop down closer to the water. It would be a wise thing to do, I take it; for in case of accident the spill wouldn't be so bad."

"All right, Frank, just as you say," replied the other, accustomed to looking to his cousin for the words of command when an emergency or a crisis came along.

He fastened the precious glasses in their rigid case, where they would be safe so long as the aeroplane remained above the surface of the water, or did not fall to the ground in a serious wreck.

Then Andy paid attention to a number of small but very important matters that had always been given over into his charge at times like this. The Bird boys had been comrades so long that they worked together like a well oiled machine. The ball team that has played in company for a season can accomplish feats that would be utterly impossible to a nine that had been brought from various clubs, even though each player might have been a star in his respective team.

So it was with Frank and Andy; they had grown to know each other's points so well that when the moment came it often seemed as though they instinctively formed a single unit, with that exceedingly bright brain possessed by Frank doing all the piloting of the combination.

They were all ready for the business in hand long before the border of the big water was reached. Frank had looked around him several times, and his cousin seemed to know instinctively that he was endeavoring to decide as to whether the wind was apt to hold as it chanced to be at the time; or increase in velocity, should they drop to lower levels.

It was rather awe inspiring to see that vast gulf of glistening water stretching as far as the eye could reach in three directions, north, east and west. From the high altitude which they still occupied, they could not tell whether the lake was calm, or waves rolling along its surface. The westering sun glittered from its bosom as though it might be streaked with gold, and altogether it was a sight that neither of the boys would soon forget.

To Andy in particular it appealed with vigor. His nature was more inclined to worship at the shrine of the romantic than would be the case with the practical Frank. To Andy that vast sheet of water seemed mysterious, profound, filled with secrets of argosies that were launched on its breast centuries ago, when only the bark canoes of the red men had ever been wedded to its waters. In imagination the boy could even then see the barques of the early explorers, those bold men who had pushed thither from across the ocean, and risked their lives in order to learn what the New Country held for brave hearts.

Perhaps, had he still gripped the glass in his hands, and cared to look earthward before leaving the shore for that adventurous cruise, Andy might have seen many a group of wondering people all watching the flight of those hurrying ships of the upper air currents, and even waving hats and handkerchiefs in the endeavor to attract the attention of the bold navigators, whom they supposed to be engaged in a race for a wager.

But there was now no longer time for anything like this, and all their attention must be concentrated upon the one thing that meant so much to them—the safety of the delicate craft in which they were now about to entrust their very lives for a voyage, the like of which few airmen had ever entered before.

Already had the other aeroplane sailed away, and was even now hanging over the inland sea, that lay fully four thousand feet below, its further shore hidden in what seemed to be a cloud, though it might prove to be a rising fog, fated to engulf both pursuing and pursued air craft in its baffling folds, and turn the comedy of the race into a tragedy.

"Goodbye old land!" sang out Andy, when they seemed to suddenly pass out over the water, leaving the shore of New York behind.

Frank said not a word, but no doubt his feelings were just as strong as those of his companion. And so they had now embarked on what seemed to be the last leg of the strange chase, with the future lying before them as mystifying as that fog bank lying far away to the north.

CHAPTER XXI

OVER THE BOUNDARY LINE

It was with the queerest possible feeling that Andy saw the land slipping away, and realized that they were at last launched upon the water part of the voyage.

It seemed as though they had cast loose from their safe moorings, and were adrift upon an uncharted sea. When comparing his feelings with other aviators in later times, he learned that every one of them had experienced exactly similar sensations the first time they passed out of touch of land, and found the heaving sea alone beneath them. It was a sort of air intoxication; Andy even called it sea-sickness, though doubtless most of it came from imagination alone.

"There they go, Frank!" he called out, not ten minutes later.

The land was far behind them now, and still in the other three directions they saw only the level surface of the great lake.

His exclamation was called out by a sudden change in the method of advance adopted by those in the leading aeroplane. Instead of keeping along in a direct line the biplane had uptilted and was now shooting downward in what seemed a terribly perilous way; just as though the pair of precious scoundrels had taken a notion to end the pursuit by seeking a plunge into the water.

But both boys knew differently, and that this was only a volplane, adopted by experienced and rash aviators as a means of reaching the lower air currents more rapidly than by slow spirals; or else undertaken when having engine trouble that threatens destruction.

Frank was ready to follow suit. It would not be the first time by long odds that the Bird boys had accomplished this speedy method of descending from high altitudes. There was always an exhilaration about the clever trick that appealed irresistibly to their natures; though Frank would never have attempted it unless reasonably sure that the conditions were favorable for success.

"Hold fast, Andy!" he remarked, quietly.

The hum of the motor suddenly ceased, and with its cessation the hydroplane was turned head-on toward the surface of the lake, four thousand feet below.

Down they went, plunging toward what seemed to be instant destruction; but a steady hand was at the wheel, and the pilot knew just what was necessary to do at the proper instant in order to bring this rapid descent to a stop, and right the airship on a level keel.

But there was no time just then to note what the rival aeroplane might be doing. Whether the experienced airman in charge managed to stop that downward plunge before reaching the surface of the lake; or failing went to his death, was a matter that did not concern them now, since they had their own affairs to look after.

To tell the truth, Andy's heart seemed to be in his throat as they made the drop. As yet they had never tried out the new hydroplane in a trick of this sort;

and hence really did not know just how it might act; though Frank must have been pretty confident, else he would never have attempted it.

Given the choice the Bird boys would easily have decided to descend from their lofty height by means of the much safer if slower "spirals," each circle seeing the aeroplane lower than before. But since the reckless man in the other air craft led the way, Frank had chosen to follow. He believed that he could accomplish any feat that was possible to Casper Blue, especially now that the old air navigator had a handicap in the way of a crippled arm.

The water seemed rushing up to meet them; so it looked to Andy, whose anxious gaze was fastened upon the lower depths, as they dipped down in that terrific swoop. But then, he had seen the same thing when over the land, so that in itself this did not daunt him.

"Oh!"

That exclamation seemed to be forced from Andy's lips when he felt Frank give a quick turn to the lever that caused the deflecting rudder to again resume a normal position. The drop of the aeroplane was brought to a gradual stop, and when immediately afterwards the buzz of the motor announced that the propelling power was again at work, it was no wonder that the nervous boy expressed his relief by giving vent to that cry. There was a world of gratitude back of that word, it can be set down as certain; for no matter how confident Andy might have been concerning his cousin's ability to accomplish wonders, the new hydroplane was as yet untried in many things.

Now he even dared take his awed gaze from the heaving waters beneath the framework of the aeroplane, and give a thought to those whom they had chased overland and water for nearly three hours.

"Bully for Casper Blue! He made the riffle too! he's all to the good!" was the way the impulsive Andy announced his discovery to Frank, who just then could not spare even a second to take his attention off the working of the motor.

After all, it was not so very strange that the boy should express himself in this way. True, the man he was praising was now a criminal, and they sought to effect his arrest in some manner as yet vague and uncertain; but it was not in this light Andy viewed him just then. As a birdsman Casper Blue had proved that he still possessed the nerve and skill to direct a daring flight, and that all the tricks known to celebrated fliers were at his finger's ends.

Any one who has risked his life up among the clouds must always respect such a valiant spirit, even though aware that the object of his admiration has in other ways forfeited the esteem of all honorable men.

There was the biplane moving along on a level keel, and not more than two hundred feet above the water. And still the course held due north, showing that the desperate men who were thus fleeing from arrest had not the slightest intention of changing their plans.

"What do you think of her now, Andy?" asked the pilot, with a quiver of pride in his voice.

"You must mean our new craft, I take it, Frank; and I want to say that she's a real peach, if ever there was one. We never volplaned as easy as that in our lives, and that's a fact. Why, it was like sliding downhill on a sled, with never a single bump on the way. I could do that all day, and never get enough."

"Dangerous business, all the same," remarked Frank; "and doubly so when you don't happen to be well acquainted with your machine. A single hitch, and we would have struck the water at a terrible rate."

"But all the same we didn't, Frank," the other went on, jubilantly; for now that this peril was of the past Andy could be his old self again.

"And they did just as well," remarked Frank, always ready to give credit, even though it might be to a rival, for his nature was generous to a fault.

"Well, that biplane was easier to manage than our hydroplane, with the pontoons underneath," Andy went on to say, grudgingly; for no one could ever convince him that Frank had his superior as an air pilot; and he would sooner go up to a record height of fifteen thousand feet in company with his cousin, than accompany the most famous man living.

"It looks like we might be booked for Canada, Frank," he went on to say, a minute later, after they had fallen into the new "stride" comfortably, and were rushing forward on a level stretch, with the surface of the lake close at hand.

"I shouldn't wonder," came the noncommital reply.

Now, Andy knew his cousin like a book. Perhaps it was something in the words; or on the other hand there may have been an undercurrent of doubt in the way Frank spoke, that aroused the other's suspicion.

"What is it, Frank?" he demanded, "for I reckon you see something that is all a blank to me? Take me in, won't you?"

"Oh! I was wondering what would happen if they had an accident away out on the lake, that's all," admitted the other.

"Well, in that event I guess it'd be up to the Bird boys to play the rescuer act for all it was worth. But Frank, do you think this new machine of ours could climb up off the water with four aboard? Wouldn't that be the limit?"

"To tell you the truth, Andy, I don't know, because we've never had the chance to try it out. With only two of us aboard you know how easy she climbed; three passengers she could hoist, but four might faze her. We can only wait and see, if ever the chance comes to make the test."

"But you wouldn't hesitate about trying the same, I know, Frank?"

"Of course not," the other remarked, confidently, "and especially when it might mean life or death to a poor fellow away out here on the lake miles from land. If we couldn't rise, we might still be able to float like a duck, and hope that some boat would come to the rescue. In the end that would be just the same."

"Do you know," said Andy, "I saw a tug pulling out at full speed from the little city on the shore of the lake, close to where we left land; and somehow I seem to have an idea they know all about us, and mean to keep in touch with us as long as they can, to be handy in case of accident. Perhaps, now, my message was phoned to Bloomsbury; and seeing about where we must be heading if we kept on a northerly course, they have wired up here to watch out for us. How about that, Frank; am I silly to figure that way?"

"I don't see why you should be, Andy. In fact, just as soon as you mentioned about the tug I began wondering if somehow these good people didn't know who we were, and what we were chasing after the biplane for."

They had to speak unusually loud in order to hear, even though their heads were close together at the time; for the propellers were whirling with a hiss, and the hum of the motor added to the noise. But then, it was all a merry racket that chimed in well with the spirit of the young aviators; and which gave them much the same pleasure that the splash through the foaming water of a ninety-foot racing yacht must awaken in the heart of an enthusiastic skipper, when he knows that every sail is drawing to the limit, and all things are working well.

"Have you figured out what we ought to do if by good luck we all get over to the other side, safe and sound?" went on Andy.

"We'll have to leave that," was the reply Frank made. "No use crossing a bridge till you come to it, you know, Andy."

"But they'll be safe then, Frank?" "I'm afraid so, even if I don't pretend to be up in all the international law connected with the passing of a thief from United States territory to Canada."

"But ain't that a measly shame?" ejaculated the indignant Andy, "to think of a robber being able to turn, and put his fingers to his nose and wiggle 'em at us, just because he happens to cross the boundary line. It oughtn't to be that way, Frank!"

"Of course not; and I guess lots of abler chaps than you and me have thought the same; but there it stands, and the two countries won't get together to change the law even a little bit. Every year dozens of embezzlers light out across the border for Canada, where they can spend their money, and start for Europe if they feel like it."

"Then perhaps it's the money they take with 'em that the Canadians like; though I wouldn't like to believe such a thing," ventured Andy.

"Hardly that; but both countries are jealous about bringing back political offenders, I've heard Judge Lawson say more than once. But don't let's talk any more'n we can help, Andy. We've got our hands full as it is watching those fellows, and keeping ready to match any trick they try."

This served to give Andy a new cause for concentrating his attention on the fleeing biplane once more. As yet the pilot of the leading airship had not diverted from his set course; but if he was as tricky as they had reason to believe, there was always a chance that he might engineer some scheme, sooner or later, looking to shaking off his pursuers here in the middle of the great lake, where possibly no mortal eye could witness the deed, so as to appear against him later on.

With the wind aft, of course the further they advanced the larger grew the waves; and Andy noticed that they were now of quite respectable size; though being directly above, he could not tell much about it, only that in many spots he saw the white caps breaking, and this served as a pointer.

Would the hydroplane be able to ride such a sea in safety, in case necessity compelled them to alight upon its swelling bosom?

Frank did not seem to doubt it, for he had the utmost confidence in the ability of those aluminum pontoons to sustain a great weight without sinking. What they would possibly have to fear more than anything else, was the chance of a capsize; and of course this would spell disaster as much as anything else.

Once they overtook a sailing schooner that was speeding along with a fair breeze. Possibly those aboard thought they were making most excellent time, with everything in their favor, but the aeroplanes sped past the vessel almost as though it were a toy craft.

A faint cheer was heard from those aboard who could be seen wildly waving head-gear, or red handkerchiefs; just as though what they considered a novel air race had been engineered especially for their amusement.

When Andy took occasion to look backward again in a short time he was amazed to discover how far distant the sails of the schooner seemed. And it was this incident more than anything else that gave him to understand just what amazing speed the aeroplanes were putting in their mad race across the inland sea.

But while up to now the voyage had been without incident worthy of mention, or accident of any kind, it could hardly be expected that this immunity would continue to the very end. The splendid good fortune that had hovered over both airships was apt to be brought to a sudden termination at any moment, as Frank well knew.

CHAPTER XXII

A HYDROPLANE RESCUE

All this while Andy's nerves had been strained to a high pitch. And it was not at all singular, therefore, that when the anticipated event came to pass he gave vent to a loud cry.

"Looky! Frank; they're going to drop! Something must have happened to the motor or else a plane guy broke to cripple them!" was what he almost shrieked.

Frank was watching, though he had not uttered a single sound. He knew that the half expected crisis was now upon them. At least his heart found cause for rejoicing that if an accident had to happen, it affected the other aeroplane rather than their own. It is much easier to bear watching another's troubles than to bear your own.

What Andy had said was the truth, for the craft they were chasing after had taken a sudden dip, and was fluttering downward.

If you have ever seen a crippled bird trying hard to keep afloat, you can have a pretty good conception of how that biplane dropped lower and lower toward the water.

That it did not fall like a lump of lead spoke volumes for the magnificent management of the pilot who controlled the levers, and whose long experience had taught him just what to do in such a dreadful emergency as this.

Frank had instantly cut off much of their power, though they still continued to sweep onward toward the place of the catastrophe, and were rapidly drawing near the falling aeroplane.

Both boys stared at the terrible picture of the descending biplane nearing the heaving surface of the lake. It seemed very serious indeed, for any one to drop in this way; and yet how much more dangerous to fall upon land, where the wrecked aviators would stand a good chance of broken limbs, even though they saved their necks.

Then a cry from the impulsive Andy told that the biplane was in the water. If the engine had broken loose there was a pretty fair chance that the craft with its long extended planes would float, and even bear up the two aviators. Perhaps the quick-witted Casper Blue had looked out for just such a contingency, and found a way to free the framework from the dead weight of the motor.

Frank had all he could do to manipulate his own craft, for in order to alight successfully, even as a wild duck does, he must make a turn, and head up into the wind.

That meant the passage of a certain length of time; and meanwhile who could say what might not be happening to the imperiled men?

On the other hand, Andy could not tear his horrified gaze away from the wreck of the fallen biplane; and it was really upon him that the navigator must depend for his information as to how things were going.

Fortunately Andy could talk as well as look; no matter if his tongue did show a decided inclination to cleave to the roof of his mouth with horror, he managed to find a way to make it wag.

"It floats, Frank, sure it floats!" he ejaculated, presently, even as the other was in the act of making a sweeping curve, and skilfully ducking a squally puff of wind, turn back over the course they had just covered, to sink down upon the heaving waters when he found the chance. "Yes, they must have kicked the engine overboard. That makes three poor old Perc has lost, don't it? There they are, both of 'em, squattin' in the middle of the wreck, just as cool as you please, awaitin' for us to call in and take 'em off. Hope it don't sink before we c'n get back. If either one can't swim they'd go down like a stone. Now you're around, Frank; and we're heading straight for the place. Hurrah! Hold hard there and we'll lend you a helpin' hand!"

He even waved toward the two men by now pretty well submerged in the water, but who seemed to be still clinging to the floating aeroplane, as though recognizing that their position might be much more desperate should they cut loose from that buoy.

Frank was watching closely, to pick out a favorable opportunity to alight. Well did he know the chances he and his chum were taking in thus dropping upon the heaving surface of such a tremendous body of water as Lake Ontario. It was true that they had successfully performed this operation many times with their other hydroplane, but that was upon the much calmer waters of little Sunrise Lake, where the sea never arose heavy enough to imperil the floating aircraft. It would be much more perilous now, under these conditions; but Frank had made up his mind to attempt the rescue of those in the water, and was not to be easily daunted.

When the right opening came he allowed the hydroplane to dip gently down, making sure that there was as little violence as possible in the drop, because of the chance of burying the forward propeller under; or losing his balance, upon which so much depended.

Andy knew what he was expected to do, and was nimbly endeavoring to swing his weight this way or that after they had launched on the waves, so as to keep the pontoons on an even keel, and prevent a disastrous spill. For once this occurred, the hydroplane would be of little more advantage than the wrecked biplane, which barely upheld the two clinging men, and was evidently sinking lower under the strain, with each passing second, until the end must be in sight.

At least they had dropped safely. The pontoons had been cleverly adjusted so as to bear a just proportion of the weight, and they did their duty faithfully and well in this great crisis.

Of course, the next thing was to try and work closer to the sinking biplane, and take the men aboard, one at a time. That would be a risky proceeding, requiring all the skill that Frank could bring to the front.

In the first place he had chosen to drop beyond the wreck of Percy's biplane. This he had purposely done, in the hope that the wind might drift them down upon the other aircraft.

A minute's observation convinced Frank, however, that if they waited for this to happen, the frail support which was buoying Casper Blue and his mate up would have gone under long long before they could get within touch.

Already the second man was shrieking for them to hurry, because he could feel himself slowly but surely sinking; and he let them know that he could not swim a stroke.

Plainly, then, they must do something to quicken things, if they meant to be of any service to the two rogues, thus brought to a sudden halt just when escape had seemed most bright.

Frank remembered his engine. But would it work under such strange conditions as this? He quickly saw that the rear propeller was half buried in the water; and if it turned at all would have to churn things just as though they were in truth a queerly fashioned boat, instead of an airship, intended to mount to lofty heights, and vie with the eagle in his circling above the clouds.

Quickly, then, he started to make the trial; and Andy, seeing his movement, comprehended what he must have in mind; for he swung out in such fashion as to preserve a balance, and thus help things along as far as lay in his power.

What a sensation of relief that hum of the faithful little Kincaid engine brought in its train, as it once more took up the burden of its busy song. Why, it seemed to Andy as though he could almost shout in sudden relief, when he heard it first, and saw the water flying from the partly submerged propeller.

But Frank was wise enough not to turn on full speed, knowing what a terrific strain this condition of affairs must be upon the entire fabric, flimsy at best; and if anything gave way it was all over with them; for if a chain is only as strong as its weakest link, a heavier-than-air flying machine certainly comes under the same category.

"We're going it, Frank!" shouted Andy, when he saw that their speed had increased several hundred per cent, and that they were now heading straight for the partly submerged air navigators.

It never occurred to Andy that either of the men might offer the slightest objection to being rescued. Frank looked a little further ahead; but even he could hardly believe that Casper Blue would prefer to drown rather than be saved.

What Frank was really concerning himself about more than anything else was how he could stow away the two fellows, once they found a chance to climb aboard the hydroplane; and whether he could get enough impetus from the engine with such an unusual load, to rise from the water, once he elevated his planes.

"Hurry! oh! Hurry! I'm going down!" cried the larger man.

Casper never said a word. Possibly, being a swimmer, he did not feel the same degree of terror that his companion experienced. Then again, he may have been coolly figuring on how he might turn the rescue to his own advantage in some way; for he seemed to have that little black box slung over his back by means of the strap; and it was easy to understand that it must, as Andy had guessed, contain something of considerable more value than a mere camera.

Now they were closing in. The hydroplane round-up was being carried out in what seemed to be a successful manner; and if all went well during the next few minutes the drifting fugitives would be hauled aboard by Andy, who stood ready to act the part of gallant rescuer to the king's taste.

It happened by mere accident that they were on that side of the sinking wreck where the larger man clung; and this was just as it should have been, since he seemed more in need of help, at least in far greater distress of mind, than the smaller man.

"Get ready, Andy!" warned the pilot; "I'll shut off the power if it seems best; but it may keep us on a more even keel if we move along."

"I'm going to try and get hold, and then pull him aboard; hope we don't have a spill, though!" the other sent back, as he braced himself as best the conditions allowed.

Frank gave one little turn to the rudder, for he was afraid that they might get past without coming in reach. Then the gap was completed, and Andy, leaning over, managed to get hold of the sinking man by the collar of his coat.

There was where the greatest danger lay.

When a man or a boy has the terror of drowning pressed in upon his heart, he is usually a most unreasonable being; and will even clasp his intended rescuer about the neck, and prevent him from carrying out his plans that might have worked well only for this blundering.

"Take it easy, you!" yelled Andy, as he saw the man clutch hold of the framework of the hydroplane, and struggle desperately to work his way along to where the others were. "If you give us half a chance we'll save you, all right; but upset us and well all like as not go down together. Slower, I tell you, or I'll give you this to teach you something. This ain't an ocean liner, d'ye understand. Let up!"

Whether it was the excited words of the boy, the manner in which he flourished that short steel bar, or his ferocious looks, that brought the excited man to his senses no one could ever say; but he did relax some of his frantic movements and began to act more within reason.

This presently gave Andy the opportunity he wanted to stretch out a helping hand, and get a firm grip of the other's coat collar; after which he exerted himself to the utmost to assist him to climb aboard.

What with his own weight, and the fact that his clothes were dripping with water, the addition of the new passenger caused the delicately constructed and already heavily freighted hydroplane to sink more deeply.

Frank, in that supreme moment realized that it would be almost a hopeless task to think of once more flying, with such a cargo aboard. Possibly the best they could do would be to keep afloat, and hope that the pursuing tug might come up with them before the darkness set in; and they could all be rescued.

Now that the first of the imperiled airmen had been hauled aboard, there remained but Casper Blue himself. The wreck had not as yet sunk wholly, since, relieved from the weight of the heavy man, it seemed to possess enough buoyancy to remain on the surface of the water. But this could be only for a short time; the planes would soon be thoroughly soaked, and then the end must come, when the clinging man would find himself deprived of all support, and must swim or go down.

He had something of a half defiant look on his small sunburned face, as he saw Andy trying to draw the wreck toward him, with the evident intention of giving him the next opening. Perhaps he was half inclined to take his chances as he was, rather than allow these two boys to make him a prisoner.

Frank had his mind made up. He figured that both men had been long enough in the water to have their weapons well soaked, so that they would be in no condition to threaten their rescuers.

"The box, make him pass it up first, or we leave him here!" he called out to Andy, as the latter was about to reach out and lay hold of the smaller man.

Casper Blue glared almost savagely at Frank. For the moment the Bird boys even thought the enraged man would hurl defiance back at them, and declare that he preferred taking his chances with the wreck rather than give up the spoils.

But just then it happened, fortunately, that the remnant of the biplane began to settle more positively than before, warning him that it was folly to pin any hope on its buoying him up more than a few minutes at most.

"Here, take it!" he snarled, handing up the box; which Andy immediately passed over to his cousin before he would stretch out his hand again to render the defeated yeggman any assistance.

Then Casper Blue was drawn aboard, and lower still sank the buoyant hydroplane, until both propellers were almost wholly submerged beneath the surface of the heaving billows that came rolling on, steadily and remorselessly.

CHAPTER XXIII

BROUGHT TO BOOK—CONCLUSION

"What time is it, Frank?" asked Andy, who was breathing very hard after his recent exertions in helping both men to get a footing on the hydroplane.

"I think pretty close to four o'clock," replied the other, though he made no attempt to take out the little nickel watch, he always carried nowadays.

The fact of the matter was that Frank did not dare trust Casper Blue. He could see that the little man was a desperate character, and that he did not view the prospect of being made a prisoner, and taken back to Bloomsbury with any great show of enthusiasm. In fact, it was a most unpleasant proposition for the bank thief to contemplate at all.

And so Frank was watching him closely. He had, before starting on this dangerous air flight that had ended so far from home, and under such singular conditions placed a little pistol in his pocket, though hardly under the belief that he would have any occasion to make use of it.

But he was now determined not to let this man get the upper hand. He could see that various desperate plans must be forming in that scheming brain of the one-time aviator, and now yeggman; and Frank was constantly on the watch so that he might not be caught napping.

"Four o'clock!" repeated Andy; "that would mean at least two more hours before the sun set, wouldn't it; and even after that it might stay light enough another hour for them to see us if they steamed along?"

"You mean the people aboard that tug, don't you?" asked Casper Blue, sneeringly.

"Yes, they seemed to be chasing after us, and I only hope they do keep moving," replied Andy, "because they must have seen the accident, that is if they had any sort of a marine glass aboard, which I reckon they did."

"And I suppose, now, you think there might be officers aboard that same tug?" the other went on to say.

"Oh! we don't know anything about that," Andy remarked, carelessly. "But if they came along after a while it'd save us from a lot of worrying. Just think, if the night set in, and the four of us weighing this poor old hydroplane down like we are what a time we'd have before another morning came around."

"It would like as not rise, if there was only two aboard, wouldn't it?" Casper asked quickly, and before Andy could understand what his question meant he had replied to it.

"Sure thing, Frank and myself have left the water many a time in a less powerful hydroplane than this, haven't we, Frank?"

"Well, turn about is only fair," said Casper, fiercely.

"Why, I don't understand what you mean by that," complained Andy.

"Two's company, four a crowd; so please skip out of this, both of you boys. My pal and me can run this shebang, and just take my word for it, we mean to do the same. Get that straight, both of you? Now, jump, I tell you, and lively, or

I might be tempted to let her go; and that would be a shame after the way you rescued the two of us. Overboard with you!"

Andy gaped when he saw that the man had actually drawn out a revolver, and was aiming the same directly at him.

"Here, quit that, will you?" he demanded, feeling a flush of alarm, for even a seasoned veteran of many battles does not fancy having such a threatening weapon thrust under his nose.

"Jump, then, d'ye hear, consarn you?" shouted the man, menacingly waving his pistol; "take a header, and over you go, both of you! I'm a desperate man, and not to be fooled with. P'raps you c'n keep afloat on that wreckage long enough for the tug to come up, and pull you in. But no matter, over you go, one way or the other!"

"Just wait a bit, Casper," said a quiet voice, and turning his head the man saw that Frank had him covered very neatly, "you must know that your weapon has been soaked, and wouldn't go off, the chances are. Besides, I don't believe there's a single cartridge in the chambers. Throw it overboard, do you hear, Casper, or I may be tempted to cripple that other arm of yours!"

No doubt Frank was speaking the exact truth when he declared his belief that the revolver had not been charged since the time when Casper emptied it at the pursuing airship, in the hope of either frightening the boy aviators; or else doing some sort of damage.

He stared hard at Frank for half a minute; then with some muttered words, as if he realized the folly of butting up against fate, threw the useless weapon far out on the heaving surface of the lake.

After that a dense silence fell upon them. The men were too down-hearted to want to talk; and there was little that the boys had to communicate, because they were now in a position where they could do absolutely nothing to help themselves; and must depend entirely upon the coming of the tug.

An hour passed, and it seemed very long. All of them were more or less wet because of the splashing waves; but as the air was balmy, they cared little for such a thing as that, if only the tug would show up.

Innumerable times did Andy stretch his neck, and look toward the quarter in which it must appear, if it came at all; but the hour began to extend far into a second one, and as yet there was nothing seen that brought with it a ray of hope.

Worse still the sea was gradually getting more and more tempestuous, it seemed to Andy, though the sky remained absolutely clear, and, there was not a sign of a storm.

If that had been a fog in the far distance which Frank had sighted, the breeze must have long ago dissipated it entirely.

Lower sank the sun, until it was now not more than half an hour above the horizon, if its stay could be measured in the way of minutes and seconds. Oh! if only the friendly tug would come in sight amidst the foam-crested waves! It was really getting to be too much of a good thing, trying to keep the hydroplane from keeling over, with those waves breaking against the frail planes. If this kept up much longer, Frank was very much afraid that Percy Carberry would not be the only boy in Bloomsbury to mourn the loss of an airship.

When, therefore, Andy gave a sudden shout, and announced that he believed he had seen the smoke of the tug wreathing above the waves, all of them looked considerably relieved, even Casper himself; for on second thoughts the yeggman must have decided that it was better to be alive and in prison, than dead, and under the waters of Lake Ontario.

In five minutes they could all see the smokestack of the powerful tug, and for fear lest it should pass by and not do them any good they shouted hoarsely in unison.

"They hear us!" exclaimed Andy, whose position, somehow, allowed him to see better than any of the others, "yes, they've changed their course, and are heading this way now. It's all right, Frank; we've won out, I guess!"

But Frank was keeping an eye on the two men. He did not mean to give them even the slightest chance to play a trick in the eleventh hour. Frank Bird was a pretty hard fellow to catch napping, he usually had his eyes open, and especially when he knew there was danger around.

The tug came booming on, and they could see that there were quite a number of people aboard.

"What if some of them are from Bloomsbury?" suggested Andy. At which his cousin laughed.

"You didn't stop to think twice before you made that break, Andy," he remarked. "Tell me, by what conveyance could they have got to the lake ahead of us, when we came through by lightning express at the rate of nearly a hundred miles an hour at times? But I can see they are expecting to take charge of our friends here, because there's an officer aboard. Just keep where you are, Casper; your goose is cooked, and there's no need of making matters worse."

The man settled back again with a growl, and then burst out into a reckless laugh.

"Small difference it makes, I guess, boys, how the thing's done, so long as we've got to go to the lock-up. You might just as well have the credit for the job as anybody; and man to man, now I want to say that I'm full of admiration for the fine way you handled that hydroplane of yours. If so be you're the Bird boys I've been hearing so much about, you've got the making of crack-a-jack aviators in you. That's about all from me now."

The tug came alongside, and the two men were assisted aboard, where the police officer saw that they were promptly ironed.

"We got the word from Bloomsbury, and your father hired this tug right away, Andy Bird, to follow you out on the lake, if so be you kept after the rascals," said a tall gentleman with a white mustache, who, they afterwards learned, was the mayor of the city on the lake shore. "Now what can we do for you?"

"Please stand by, and let's see if we can get away," answered Frank, "if not we'll have to go on board, and tow the hydroplane behind, but since relieved of so much extra weight the pontoons have risen again; and I expect she'll go."

And she did, with the very first effort, beginning to move over the surface of the water in the lee of the tug; then, as Frank hastened to elevate the planes, the airship started to mount and when free from the lake a mighty cheer broke from the lips of those aboard the small vessel, even Casper Blue joining in giving the brave lads their just dues.

Frank carefully started back toward the American side of the lake. He did not know whether the capture had been made on the Canadian side or not, and as the question was never raised, even in the trail of the bank robbers it was never wholly clear in his mind.

When they reached land it was early night; and save that the wind had lulled considerably, they would not have been able to get in for a long time after that. As there was no need of their hurrying homeward, Frank and Andy consented to stay over as the guests of the mayor, who was more than pleased to have the famous Bird boys stop under his roof.

But first Frank made sure to send a message to each of their homes; as well as to Chief Waller, who would have to come on and get the two bold men who had broken into the Bloomsbury bank and about cleaned out the vault; and not content with one haul, were planning to rob the pay-car when it stopped in Bloomsbury to settle with a large number of employees centering there.

Doubtless that must have been a season of considerable excitement in the home town; and the names of Frank and Andy Bird were cheered to the echo by the crowds of town boys Larry and Elephant would lead around, burning red lights and firing off Roman candles purchased with money supplied by Dr. and Professor Bird, the happy fathers of the two young heroes.

On the following day Chief Waller was on hand with one of his men to escort the prisoners back to the town where their latest crime had been committed. Frank had already sent the little camera box with its valuable contents, just as he had received it from Casper Blue, to the president of the bank by express, not caring to hold it any longer in his hands than was absolutely necessary.

About noon, the conditions being favorable, the Bird boys sailed away amidst the cheers of half the little city, and headed directly south on a bee line for home.

Fortunately enough no further adventures overtook them on their way there, and as their coming had been announced they found the whole town in an uproar, and came near being mobbed, such was the desire of every man, woman, boy and girl to have the honor of shaking hands with them.

Percy was on hand too, with a thousand questions concerning the fate of his precious biplane, and bemoaning the fact that he seemed to be the most unlucky fellow who had ever attempted to bring honors to Bloomsbury. But there were precious few who sympathized with him; and everybody knew that all he had to do was to demand that his mother advance the ready cash to buy another flier, and it was sure to be forthcoming.

But there were other lively times in store for Frank and Andy Bird, although neither of them suspected it just then, and believed that a period of calm would likely follow their hydroplane round-up. What the nature of these exploits were the reader who has accompanied us in our voyage through the pages of this book, will learn when he purchases the next story in this series, now on sale under the title of "The Bird Boys' Aeroplane Wonder or, Young Aviators On a Cattle Ranch."

Lightning Source UK Ltd.
Milton Keynes UK
29 October 2010

162091UK00001B/134/A